A novel by J. J. Gould

© J. J. Gould
Published 2017

ISBN-13: 978-1975817732

ISBN-10: 1975817737

Acknowledgements

Others may have a host of helpers to acknowledge- I have one. This book would not be written, edited or published without a lot of free and patient advice from Tamara Blodgett. Thank you!!

Prologue

His vacation turned out to be quite productive after all. Dormeier wasn't much of a hunter, but a buddy who used to play for the Knicks had told him about the pheasants in South Dakota, so he went along. The trip was a mix of highs and lows—a lot of well-heeled guys in brand-new Cabella's camo with Benellis they'd probably never even shot before. But it was still okay. It was the end of October, and the sky was the kind of brilliant blue that made it hard to focus on anything close by. He was not used to how far away the horizon was and found himself taking deep breaths, searching for the familiar smell of civilization, but there wasn't any, just sky and prairie, the trucks small and insignificant parked at the far edge of the field. Dormeier was a big man, and the fame and money of his career made him even bigger, but the vast prairie pressed down on him and made him seem insignificant, a feeling he did not like.

But the birds were everywhere, and soon Dormeier got the knack, like he always did, and shooting the birds out of the sky gave him the measure of power and control he was used to.

Afterwards the lodge was stocked with top-shelf booze and some hookers from nearby—some of whom were so young they didn't yet realize they were hookers, but that was okay too.

But the productive part came that night as he overheard some of the local guys trying to impress the rich and famous. He caught a bit of the conversation going on behind him:

"…burned to a crisp, all four of 'em."

"Is that what killed 'em?"

"Probably. How should I know? I'm just an undertaker."

"I thought you said you were the county coroner —"

"I am the county coroner—been that for twelve years."

"Don't you have to be a doctor or somethin'?"

"Nahh—not here. You just gotta get elected—and who else wants to drive around at all hours fishing stiffs out of sloughs and burnt cars?"

"What if someone gets murdered?"

The man laughed. "In Dansing? Not likely. Anyway, if it looks suspicious, we can ship a body to Rapid or Sioux Falls to a coroner there. Like if the guy's been shot. Sometimes, the family is all paranoid, so they'll pay to have an autopsy if they want."

"So what if someone keels over while they're driving on the interstate?"

"Same thing. If the family wants an autopsy, they can have one. Most of the time they don't."

Fascinated, Dormeier fought the urge to turn around and join the conversation. Instead he stared into the fireplace and tried to imagine a place where people died and nobody seemed to care how *they died.*

Hmm.

It was something to think about.

Friday
Chapter 1 - Stan

The wind. Always the wind.

This time it came out of the north at about twenty miles an hour, blowing shards of snow and tumbleweeds across miles of emptiness, until it reached the main street of Dansing, South Dakota. What buildings there were didn't slow the wind down much; in a few short blocks it continued on its way south, leaving a few tumbleweeds behind, whirling along its empty streets. It was the end of March, technically spring, but the wind had a bite that burned bare skin. An ironic drift of snow collected on the edge of the display window of Amada's Klassy Klothes, where, inside, shadowed mannequins wore shorts and swimsuits. They looked cold.

At 5:25 in the morning, there was little sound and certainly no traffic: the metallic clanging a rope makes when it's banging against a flagpole; the wind, of course; and the rhythmic click the three stoplights on Main Street made as the lights changed, directing traffic that wasn't there.

Red. *Click*. Green. *Click*. Yellow. *Click*.

Two blocks from the radio station, a lone man rounded the corner, running. His breath came out in ragged puffs of white, then was whipped away by the wind in his face. He lurched and caught himself on the trunk of a parked car, bent over, and retched. Thin and yellow, the vomit smelled of acid and alcohol, but the smell, too, was carried off by the wind.

Stan was late. Sign on was at 5:30. Wiping his jaw with the back of his hand as he ran, he reached for the keys in his pocket out of reflex. The battered white steel door at the back of the building was the one the jocks used. Three months before, a strong wind had blown the door open and sprung the hinges, and now it couldn't be closed, much less locked. Now the wind had slammed it open again, and it banged angrily against the back of the building. A small drift of snow trailed into the back of the wide-open building. After the door had broken, Stan had reported it and was ignored. That morning the broken door was fine. Perfect. *Every second counts when you're late.*

He flicked on a light and pulled the door closed in the same motion. He fastened it with a bungee cord wrapped around the handle and hooked thru an eyebolt screwed into the doorframe. He stepped through a small pile of snow toward the rack of radio equipment. The room

was still cold, and the fluorescent light was blue and flickering. The wind still whistled through the sprung doorframe, but the furnace was hard at it, its noise and warmth drowning out most of the outdoor noise.
Above the rack hung yellowed, typewritten instructions, taped there a long time before by a forgotten engineer. *Step One: Engage black button and allow filaments to warm up for one minute. Step Two: Engage red plates button and turn on transmitter. Step Three: Check VU meter for proper readings.*

Stan knew these by heart, of course. These were the steps for turning on the transmitter and beginning another broadcast day. He slapped the black button and ran down the hallway while the plates were warming up. He flicked on lights as he ran into the copy room. Yellow paper had been pooling off the wire into a pile on the floor since midnight. He ripped the copy off the Teletype and headed back to the transmitter rack, a stream of wire copy trailing behind.

He punched the red button, and the needle jumped, faltered, then steadied. The static on the monitor stopped, and the silence meant that KDAN was broadcasting dead air.

Stan stopped and heaved again into a wastebasket. The smell of vodka and grapefruit juice was immediate.

No time. Deal with it later.

Still trailing yellow paper behind him, Stan headed to the control room, flicked on a light, grabbed a battered cart off the top of the rack, slammed it into the cart deck at exactly 5:30:15, and hit the start button. The cart deck was the third one and was broken. In fact, all four cart decks were broken. Each deck had its own frustrating issues that made a professional broadcast impossible. Deck number three had a rubber capstan wheel so hard and slippery, no cart with more than forty seconds of tape in it would play without dragging. Sure enough, the tape made a wowing sound as the music climbed up to speed. "Good Mornin'" with Shirley Jones and Frank Sinatra woke up Dansing for the millionth time. An earlier program director had attempted to replace the song, but Alice Ronseth, who owned the Edge o' Town motel, had complained. Finally she offered to *sponsor* the song each morning, and that ended that. The music played for thirty seconds, then Bill Conley's voice started in. He'd left about three years ago, but the cart was still good, so nobody bothered changing it. For forty-two seconds he greeted Dansing in a cheery singsong, welcoming them to another KDAN broadcast day chock-full of news, sports, weather (of course weather), and farm market reports all serving the fine people of Dansing and the entire west central region. He ended by thanking the Edge o' Town ("wake up to a gre-eat mornin' at the Edge o' Town motel!") Twenty-three seconds of music with a hard outro followed, then dead air.

Fortunately, Stan understood radio and had been there before. He knew how to handle out-of-breath late and drunk and puking sick.

Still gasping for breath, he dashed into the on-air studio and grabbed a pair of beat-up headphones (eighty-dollar Sennheisers from before The Fall) bound together with duct tape. The studio was a depressing combination of chipped imitation-wood Formica and faded, red shag carpet. It smelled of years of stale cigarette smoke mixed with the new tang of vomit, sweat, and alcohol.

He slammed a random cart off the rack and into the cart machine just as the music stopped, turned on the mic, and potted it up. "Good morning, this is Stanley Martin welcoming you to another Friday, the last day of March"—he clicked off the mic for a split second to exhale and grab another quick breath—"a brisk late-winter morning, and your complete forecast is next." He clicked off the mic again and fired the cart machine, triggering the commercial to play. *Good, it's a 60.* Usually, no spots were scheduled between 5:30 and 6:00 a.m., but bonus spots were okay, and sometimes—like this morning—absolutely necessary.

Still catching his breath, Stan quickly scanned and sorted the copy into piles, using the hard edge of the counter next to the board to rip the twenty-foot sheet of paper into individual stories. His eyes caught the headline: Regional Forecast and Current Temps. *Good.* He ripped and stacked that by the mic. *Ten seconds.* He kept breathing deep, trying to get on top of his oxygen debt. His eyes were bloodshot, he was unshaven, a streak of drying vomit was trailing down his sweatshirt, and his hair was matted with sweat. But Stan was doing radio, and no one could see all that.

All they could see was what their imaginations told them to see, and that was conveyed to them through sound alone. And that sound was the reason why firing Stanley Martin would be very hard. He had the voice of God. Thirty-eight years old but sounding eternal, deep, resonant, warm and confident. A voice that was smooth and layered with a hint of raspy texture, like honey mixed with whisky. His whole life, people had commented on his voice. But it was more than that. Stan also had the rare ability to sound as though he was talking to just you- *your* kind and good neighbor coming into *your* warm kitchen and sitting at *your* table telling *you* about the day's events and making you feel like you were being let into the confidence of some great world leader.

Catching his breath between sentences and commercials, Stan bought some time by throwing in a cart with Dave Brubeck's "Take Five." He had a stash of carts beside the board, which he used when he didn't have time to cue up a 45 on the turntable. People not in radio didn't realize all the things he could do in thirty seconds, much less three minutes. By 5:45, he had time to toss the vomit-coated wastebasket out back by the Dumpster (he could clean it up later), wash his face and gargle, strip off his sweatshirt (he was too hot, and his sweat smelled of alcohol), and even make some coffee. But he also knew he would fool nobody.

He'd failed—again.

Sighing, he looked forward to the rest of his day with dread. Maybe that night he could sleep.

It was only 6:00 a.m.

How can you fall any lower?

****

Stan and the rest of the track team knew The Bear was right. A lot of wind that day, and no chance at a record. "The Bear" was what the team called him when he wasn't around. A big lumbering man with bad knees, he was the last guy you'd think to coach a small college track team, especially when he could barely speak the language, but there he was, against all odds, and there they were, at the Drake Relays, ready to compete against better programs.

"No," he had said when he heard the boys muttering about the expensive equipment and the luxury motor coaches surrounding them. They themselves had come in a beat-up church bus borrowed from St. Dominic's. Most had one uniform to practice and compete in, and a few had one pair of shoes to last the season.

His Slavic face was impassive, his accent thick. "Better is here." He tapped his head. "Even better is here." And he tapped his chest. That was something he said a lot. And because he believed in each member of the team, because he would look in each of their eyes, searching for the very best they could give, they believed in themselves. This strange belief carried over not only to the throwing events—he had been a long-past Olympic competitor in the shot—but also, inexplicably, to the other events. They would not win that day—could not win that day. The team had only five members, two for the shot put, discus, and javelin, one high jumper, and two runners. Yet, surprisingly, they managed to perform beyond themselves, placing well in events they had no business competing in.

Stan McGarvey was the biggest surprise. Lean and lithe with penetrating blue eyes, the kid seemed to glide along the track on legs of steel. He came in second in the half mile, a total dark horse, then got 4:04:03 in the mile—an incredible time in that wind.

The Bear lumbered over, swaying from side to side on bad knees. "Stanley." He only used a first name if the request was important.

The young man was flat on the ground, stretching his rubbery legs, breathing hard, trying to replenish the oxygen his muscles had burned up. Still catching his breath, he stood up, alert, hands on hips. "Yes, Coach?"

The Bear stood close and looked down into his eyes, measuring him. "Can you do the two-mile?" Their eyes locked for a few long seconds. The young man's eyes widened, and he gulped a little, looking away. He had never run two miles in competition, and he knew the Bear knew that. He drew a deep breath and paused. Then, he gathered himself and looked up at the coach with a gaze that many found unsettling.

He took another breath, nodded, and said simply, "Yes, sir."

Chapter 2 - Larry Karl

At 6:58 a.m., Larry Karl came in the back through the beat-up white door. He pulled it open far enough to reach in and grab the bungee cord that held it closed. As he opened it, the wind grabbed the door from his hand and slammed it against the building. That had happened many times—a hole had been punched into the cinder-block wall just the size of the doorknob. Larry swore at the door without much feeling and pulled it closed again. Above and below the door were chewed-up places where various pneumatic door closers had been tried over the years and had failed—each ripped out of place by the wind. The bungee cord worked the best over time, and only the jocks used this door anyway.

Larry sniffed the air and smiled. *Ol' Stan the Man got a little juiced last night. Should be a little exciting this morning.* Larry had been born and raised in Dansing and was a little suspicious of Stan, who wasn't From Here…- and more than a little jealous of the time Stan had spent in the major markets. Stan had never told Larry where he had worked, but Eddie the night jock said he let slip once that he worked a few years in Atlanta, Chicago, maybe Phoenix… a lot of places.

Larry's job was to run the board for Stan during the seven o'clock news hour, then from eight thirty to noon to do Karl's Korner, a show where he read farm market prices every twenty minutes, played some easy listening LP's, and generally did as little as possible. In the business, he was known as a puker, a term used for jocks who thought they sounded better with a forced singsong delivery and plugged nose.

Larry ambled into the studio just as Stan finished pulling the spots for the seven o'clock hour and stacking the carts next to the cart decks off to the right side of the board. Technically that was Larry's job, but both were okay with the current arrangement. Stan didn't like having people in his studio when he was on the air, and Larry didn't like work.

"Mornin', Big Stan!" Larry was six feet and two-sixty. Stan was about five-nine. Larry often called him Big Stan, hoping it would bug him. If it *did* bother him, Larry didn't know—Stan had an excellent poker face.

Larry sniffed the air so Stan would notice him. "What happened to *you* last night?"

"Hang on," Stan said and flipped his mic on. When that happened, the red on-air light turned on, and the monitor went silent. Every jock who had ever pulled a shift knew to shut up when the monitor was silent or risk being heard on the air. Stan's mic was on, so Larry kept his mouth shut. *Son of a bitch is avoiding me*. Thirty seconds clicked off the clock, while Larry stared at Stan, and Stan stared at the sweeping second hand. Larry was irked. *Shit*. It wasn't fair—Stan was the drunk, Stan was the one looking like a wino, and here he was calm and cool, like he was Edward R. Murrow or whoever.

Stan gave the legal ID: "You're listening to The Big Neighbor, 8-70 AM, K-D-A-N, Dansing, South Dakota." Even though Larry didn't want to, he found himself watching the sweeping second hand—five seconds left.

"It's twenty-two degrees, and at the tone, seven o'clock."

He potted up the network in time to hear an electronic *bip* followed by the Mutual Network news sounder... and another authoritative voice started telling the news of the day. *Bastard is a pro*. The thought bothered Larry more than he thought it would. With a sour expression he fell into the routine developed over a thousand mornings.

Stan pulled the plug on his cans and moved over to the news chair on the other side of the board. He sat on the other side of the fake wood countertop, where he would be what his official title was at KDAN—news director. From there, he read the news at 7:05, 7:30, and 7:55 and then would disappear to record some news. He would emerge usually within fifteen minutes with four neatly labeled carts containing news segments that were played throughout the morning.

Larry was officially known as farm director. A rural station like KDAN featured a lot of farm news, mainly so they could play spots from big ag companies. The national ad agencies that represented the ag companies had no idea how cheap spots were in South Dakota, and were gouged accordingly. As farm director, Larry's job was to run the board for Stan, rip and read the farm market reports, and read the sports. Larry was a sports legend in Dansing—played some nine-man football back in the day before the asshole coach kicked him off the team. The basketball coach was just as bad (no eye for talent), so much of Larry's sport coverage included commentary from his world-weary perspective.

Larry sniffed the air again so Stan would notice and asked again, "What happened to *you* last night?"

Stan looked at Larry with a blank gaze for a long second. "Long story… Say, Larry, I gotta clean up the wire and get my news cuts. I'll be back."

The gaze had intimidated Larry, but he didn't want to admit it, so he slurred his voice for a snappy come back. "Hookay, BigStan... but don' fallover or nuthin', hokay?"

Chapter 3 - Happy Jack

By the time Happy Jack Wilson got to the station, it was a little after eight in the morning, and most of the regular staff had arrived. Lois and Lorna worked the front desk and handled billing and traffic. Both were small, with mouse-like movements and were whispering busily when Jack walked in. Happy Jack was the general manager, an overweight middle-aged man with a comb-over and a perpetually strained smile. Even on the coldest days, his face had a sheen of sweat. The "girls," as he called Lois and Lorna, had left girlhood about forty years ago, keeping only their high school hairdos and a love for gossip. Most days they shuffled and collated the stacks of paper a small radio station generated and looked for something to disapprove of. Judging by their tight lips and eager expressions, today must be a doozy.

"Helluva day, eh, girls?" Happy Jack believed that a breezy nonchalance was the best way to handle most circumstances.

Lorna stopped her whispering to look significantly, first to Jack and then to the broadcast studio. KDAN was built in the days when radio had an element of live performance. The studio was about ten by ten, glass on two sides, and it was common back in the day to bring groups of schoolchildren in to tour the facilities. That hadn't happened for a while (now kids were taken to the TV station in Mitchell), and the glassed-in studio looked like an overgrown aquarium in need of cleaning. Through the murky glass it was still obvious that Stan was having a bad day. *Oh Jeez. Not today.*

It was no secret that the girls shared Larry Karl's distrust of Stan (he was Not From Here and drank besides) and would like nothing better than to have him fired. It was also no secret that Happy Jack was not that good of a general manager. Instead of hiring people and firing people, he preferred a simpler method when problems arose: feign ignorance and wait for things to blow over. He tried it now. Facing away from the studio, he turned to the girls.

"You going to the press conference or staying back?"

In a magnanimous gesture earlier in the week, Happy Jack had said anyone who wanted to go the Holiday Inn for the press conference (except the on-air staff) could go. It was a big deal, in a part of the world where big deals didn't happen very much. Hopefully talk of the big events of the day would derail the current situation.

The girls exchanged looks again.

Uh-oh.

Jack pretended he didn't notice and breezed back to the hallway by the studio to get a cup of coffee. The layout of KDAN was haphazard and inefficient, but at least the coffee was located where the late-night and early staff could get to it easily, right outside the studio underneath the On-Air sign. The farther away from the front door one ventured, the more dilapidated the building looked, and that morning was even worse. The smell of sweat and alcohol was obvious and radiating off of his news director, who at that moment had left the studio and was shaving some stubble off his chin over the sink outside the bathroom in a corner of the lounge. A long time before, another owner had converted a record-storage room into a lounge-type area for the jocks, complete with sink, shower, and some beat-up couches. The jocks liked it and never cleaned it—the rest of the staff avoided it if possible. Wearing rumpled khakis and a yellowed wifebeater, Stan wiped bits of shaving cream off his face and reached for a worn white dress shirt and tie. His shift was over, and he was getting ready for the press conference.

Oh jeez. Not today of all days.

Happy Jack's strained smile got wider. "Big day, huh, Stan?" Stan nodded, buttoning the shirt, looked in the cracked mirror, and avoided eye contact. He put the wrong buttons in the wrong holes and had to start over again.

Oh jeez. Oh jeez.

Happy Jack was tempted to walk closer and give a pep talk, a really good "win one for the Gipper" type, but halfway across the room the fumes discouraged him.
Maybe if Stan brushed his teeth, gargled, and put on some cologne. He knew Stan's car wasn't working—maybe that was a good thing. Walking four blocks to the Holiday Inn might give him a chance to air out.
He tried more cheeriness. "I heard a TV crew from Sioux Falls is coming out to cover it—maybe even someone from Bismarck, if the roads are good."
Nothing.

He added lamely, "That'll put Dansing on the map!"

No answer.

Happy Jack topped off his coffee and sauntered back to his office by the front door, smiling at everyone until the door was safely closed.

Oh jeez.

Chapter 4 - Stan

The press conference was scheduled for ten in the morning, at the conference centre of the local Holiday Inn. The conference centre was actually a rectangular steel box attached to the hotel with absolutely no attempt at architectural style except for the spelling of its name, but it was big enough for a couple thousand when the livestock show was in town.

Stan had hurried to get the newscasts recorded, checked the batteries in the Marantz tape deck, shouldered the deck—plus cord and mic—into the KDAN news knapsack, and headed out the door. A standing joke among the jocks went that the TV stations out of Sioux Falls and Rapid City got news vans, even a network satellite truck if they needed it, but the Big Neighbor KDAN got a news knapsack.

The wind was still at it, snapping the frayed flag by the post office, but Stan didn't mind. The fresh air was cleaning the last bits of a bad morning away, and besides, the trek was only four blocks. He left his hooded sweatshirt behind and had only a rumpled white shirt, a black tie, and khakis underneath his trench coat. His black dress shoes were the embodiment of life after The Fall. They were steel-toed mechanic's shoes he'd bought on clearance at the JC Penney store before they left town. Heavy, not stylish, they were black and affordable. The right sole had a crack in it, but that was waiting in line behind the other things that needed money until payday.

His face was red and wind burned by the time he arrived at nine forty-five, and Larry Karl had been right— two TV news crews were setting up in front of the podium, shoving Hal from the Gazette aside without so much as a glance. Hal saw Stan coming in and shot a glance at a TV reporter then looked back and rolled his eyes.

TV.

Hal wrote about seventy percent of what the *Dansing Regional Gazette* put out. His real name was Hal Steinwaller, but he always introduced himself with "Hey, I'm Hal From-the-Gazette," so that was the name that most called him.

Stan went to attach his mic to the podium. A flashy self-important blonde whirled around and flashed him a five-hundred-watt smile. "Hi, I'm Stacy Andersen, KSDU TV!"

"I'm Stanley Martin, KDAN."

"Oh." Stacy shut the smile off immediately, saving it for someone important.

She could not believe she'd drawn this assignment. Meeting a former NBA star and millionaire was cool, but the five-hour one-way trip was not. And to make matters worse the other news crew from Bismarck had gotten there before them and hogged all the outlets by the podium, and even worse yet, that reporter had on a virtually identical outfit. *Bitch*.

****

Stupid, stupid, *a small voice shouted inside his brain*. You are stupid! *For the first mile he had kept his shoulder on Jenkins, pushing him to set a fast pace and leave the pack —and now he was dying. He was a half-mile man, and he was running the two-mile. His legs were rubber, and his lungs felt as if a coarse file had been rasping against them. He could feel his muscles knotting, giving up. What had he been thinking? Why not just quit? He had nothing to prove —he couldn't win.*

"No!" *he gasped. Jenkins heard it and glanced back. They were rounding the track, and Stan could see,* feel *another runner, Hendrickson, finding a gear and closing the gap behind him.* "No!" *He gasped again— angry that time, angry that his body was weak, angry at the pain.*

"No!" *he said again. And again. Hendrickson was gaining stride by stride. One lap was left, and then he was there—he could feel Hendrickson, sense him, right behind.*

With a flood of red and a burst of pain, his mind demanded more, more, more! Then the finish line flashed

*past, and he collapsed onto the track, skidding into
unconsciousness.*

*Later, after the bus ride home, the Bear
approached him in the locker room alone. "Stanley." His
face was impassive, but there was moisture at the corner of
his eye. Stan had ice on his legs where the long scrapes
from the cinder track had rasped. He was still in some
pain, but he could deal with it. He looked up with that
penetrating gaze that made so many uncomfortable.*

*The old coach got carefully to his knees. The
locker room was empty. Gray metal locker doors were
closed, and the smell of sweat and cleanser hung in the air
like incense. The coach's face was working through a
number of emotions, his mouth puzzling for words to say.
Finally, he leaned into Stan's face, looked down into his
eyes, and with a huge gnarled finger tapped the young
man's chest gently.*

*"I—" He paused, unable to come up with a word.
He wiped his eyes and tried again. "You are… hero." He
paused, thinking about the word, then nodded.*

"Hero."

*With that said, the coach seemed to become self-
conscious. He lurched painfully to his feet and walked out,
not looking back. Stanley's gaze followed him as he left.*

*A few minutes later he shrugged and left the locker
room, limping slightly, forgetting the moment altogether
until he had cause to remember it almost twenty years
later.*

Chapter 5 - Dormeier

He might have even found it comical if he didn't have a stiff neck and a hangover. He had a stiff neck because the nearest airport was in Pierre, the capital, a village of maybe ten thousand, with a runway so miniscule no wide-body could land on it, so he was stuck in some turbo prop bush plane with a pilot that looked like he graduated from high school last year and a first-class section that consisted of two seats, 110 decibels of prop noise, and a flight attendant that looked like the pilot's prom date. He had the hangover because he always got a hangover from red wine, and that was the only thing the crummy concierge at the Pierre Holiday Inn could find him when he checked in at one o'clock that morning.

Now it was about nine in the morning. Dormeier and the rest of the group were about halfway into the two-hour drive. The ten-year-old limo squeaked and clattered over the patched road, which stretched flat and featureless off to the edge of nowhere. To emphasize the point, an honest-to-God tumbleweed blew across the road in front of the limo.

Reese got a big kick out of that. "Hey, check that out! Is that a *tumbleweed*?" Reese had been with him for years, probably the closest part of his entourage, maybe even a friend, certainly a pain in the ass. Two of Reese's irritating qualities were that he never seemed to get a hangover and he talked too much, especially in the morning.

"Lookit that shit!" Reese had finally noticed the tumbleweeds and started pointing them out, some stuck in drifts of lingering snow, others just piled up all along the fence line as far as the eye could see. Then Reese starting singing about a tumbling tumbleweed; when he started to yodel, Dormeier told him to shut up.

Shit, it was depressing. The things he did to get ahead, to gain an advantage. *Why does everything have to be so hard?* He considered how his life had taken a downward turn since the glory days. Ten years before, his picture was in Times Square, one hundred fifty feet high, but today he was schmoozing a bunch of hicks in Flyover Land. He turned the diamond-and-gold championship ring around an enormous finger absently, wondering why he needed to be here. He had already accumulated wealth, was richer than his prick of a father had ever been, but here he was out here grubbing for money. *No, not just money. Freedom.*

He glanced across the limo at Marie, the cause of his misery, staring out the window with that stupid bored expression she usually had. No, being here was not pleasant, not at all, but it was necessary, and perhaps the last unpleasant thing he would ever have to do. *And that makes everything worth it.*

He ran over the plan again. He felt for the stiff envelope of cash in his breast pocket to make sure it was still there. *Thirty thou should be enough.* The plan was simple, but even simple plans had to be executed properly. It had to be good, or the cops wouldn't swallow it. And they had to swallow it—maybe not forever but for at least a week, maybe two tops, and if he'd learned anything, the bigger the lie, the easier it was to swallow.

******

Dormeier's last season, and he was mostly just going through the motions. For nine years with the Celtics, he'd been an okay shooter, better on defense, great off the boards, and truly artistic with his elbows when the refs weren't looking. He didn't need the money—his dad owned a shipping business, and his grandmother had left him a trust when he was eighteen. But early on he'd realized being rich was good, but being rich and *famous made it easier to get richer, and being richer was definitely better. He'd also learned that as far as most people were concerned, being infamous was about as good as being famous. And he was definitely infamous—an enforcer, a guy who got paid to play dirty, and got paid pretty well.*

The truth was he liked it. Violence was funny that way. At home, behind closed doors he could get beaten with a belt by a rich and influential father, and it was called discipline. On the street, someone would be arrested for the same thing because it was called assault, but on the court it was another thing altogether. Here, he'd get a foul, maybe a technical, and fifteen seconds of fame on a highlight reel. And that night he was gunning for another fifteen seconds.

The kid was cocky. Twenty years old, dropped out of college and going to make big bucks right away. He was a second-round draft pick, a big risk who was paying off, on the way to being a top-five rookie—a lot of flash, a media darling.

A column in the sports page of the local paper talked about his rough childhood and how he was going to pay back his mom for all her sacrifices by buying her a house, and how she made sure she could be courtside at tonight's game.

How touching.

The kid (what was his name?) was tough to defend, all right; he had legs like springs and long too, like trying to run around a fence. He didn't trash talk but wore a look that said, "You tired, old man?"

That pissed Dormeier off, but he was patient, and in the middle of the third he caught the kid as he was driving the paint, lifting for a layup. Dormeier jumped a split second later and caught him in midair, their legs and arms tangled. As they fell, he twisted, locking his leg around the kid's knee.

The crack was like a rifle shot. The kid's kneecap hit first, the full weight of both of them driving it into the court. Twisting himself free, he "accidentally" wrenched the damaged knee around, messing with some tendons and cartilage.

The kid screamed, and the officials called a time out. Horrible... so horrible it would be played several times a day for the next week on TV.

As the trainers ran to the court, he took a quick moment to cradle the kid's face in his enormous hands. That shot would make it on the news too, the old veteran with a heart of gold. What the cameras didn't catch was much closer. He tenderly wiped some tears away and whispered something only the kid could hear:

"Hey, kid. Say hi to your mom for me."

Chapter 6 - Marie Dormeier

She was dead. The fact did not make her afraid or even sorry, really. In a strange way it gave her a sense of peace, relief even. For seven years she had known that her marriage to John Dormeier would not end well. She'd probably known it even before they were married. But he was a hard person to say no to, even if the end result was her misery. Not just hers—she had seen others fall into the same trap. Men seemed unable to not do whatever John wanted. His money and his fame were a big part of that. His size was another—people who got close to him seemed to shrink and lose power. It had certainly been true for her.

Funny how her life, once filled with such promise, was turning out like this. She had money, herself. And beauty. And a number of willing suitors. But when John Dormeier loomed over her that first time, he seemed to suck the air out of the room, and she was no longer in control of anything.

Her wealth was hers, in the form of stock from a wealthy grandfather. Its exact amount she didn't really know or care about—millions, maybe hundreds of millions. Frankly, it was more than she needed. The family had houses all over the place. So the money was only really used for parties and vacations and trips and whatever she needed to avoid boredom as best she could. But the money was important to John. He poured over the paperwork with lawyers and investment experts, plotting and scheming. She did not have the least bit of interest in any of it, but she did have a sense that whatever he was trying to do, he couldn't get done.

She knew money was important to him in general, and *her* money was important to him in particular, and because of the way he treated her, she also knew that for whatever reason he could not get to her money.

And then that changed. He came back from a hunting trip, somewhere out west, and he was… different. *Relaxed* wasn't the word—maybe *focused*. Like he had solved a problem and was just waiting for its resolution. And because money was all he was concerned about she knew instinctively that he must have figured out how to get hers and get away with it.

Then began a sort of waiting game. He treated her differently, almost kindly, like when he used to have to sign autographs for sick kids at the hospital. And she figured it out too, just like those sick kids did, kids who heard doctors whispering behind closed doors and figured out for themselves that they were dying. Only in her case the whisperings weren't about doctors and cancer. They were about John and money.

And murder.

Chapter 7 - Estelle

Her name was Estelle Romano, and she was among the very best imaging professionals in the country. She told her clients she was a branding consultant; she told her friends she polished turds. And that was why she had ridden to Dansing half an hour earlier, in the back of an old limo that stank of stale cigarette smoke, and avoided the creepy smile of the guy they called Reese.

She shuddered involuntarily at the memory and subconsciously pulled her skirt down half an inch as she stood behind the podium. *Should have worn the grey business suit.* The suit was probably too formal for the occasion, but it also came down to mid-calf, and it would have avoided Reese staring across the limo at her knees for two hours. *What a creep.*

She shook it off and focused on the matter at hand, looking around the Dansing Convention Centre.

Depressing. The colors were at least thirty years out of style. Dust-covered plastic plants and cheap paintings huddled in dimly lit corners. The carpet wrinkled away from the walls and smelled vaguely of spilled beer and disinfectant.

Oh well.

She shrugged her shoulders and put her game face on. Dark hair that curled in waves framed a face that was attractive enough to disarm men but wasn't so attractive to make women insecure. Her smile was warm and engaging as she invited people to sit in front of the podium for what she said was a vision of the future.

She was paid to make these visions look good, and she did. Her Chicago firm was given $75,000 for this particular vision: the ultimate hunting lodge and gaming casino. All conceptual, she was told—strictly prospectus-type stuff.

Easy.

Conceptual stuff was her bread and butter. She helped developers across the country show what a shopping mall might look like, or how great a football stadium would be before the bond issue, stuff like that. Usually these presentations involved a certain piece of land, but not this time. She was not given details about where exactly this particular casino might be—could be in town, could be out in the country. *Kinda weird.* Usually investors nailed down a piece of property first to avoid speculators bidding up the possible real estate, but whatever. The town was a dump. She had left a town a lot like it years before and had spent a lot of effort hiding the fact. Why would Dormeier want to raise money in a town that obviously had no prospects? *Oh well, it's his money.* She stepped to the podium. *Show Time.*

The lights dimmed, and a video played:

A collage of shots—a prairie thunderstorm rolling across the plains, prairie grass waving in an impossibly beautiful blue sky, a herd of cattle grazing as the sun set, badlands in the background. Then a Sam Elliot sound-alike said: *"This is the heartland: a place of vast skies and endless prairie, a place where a man can dream big and live free. And no matter where life may take him, he still comes back to hang his hat at The Grand Prairie."* The music swelled up from under the voice as the shots changed to cutaways of opulent hunting lodges, luxurious gaming tables, beautiful girls lounging by pools, beautiful girls lounging at bars, and beautiful girls lounging at romantic dinner tables. After ten minutes of that, the music crescendoed as a logo displayed: ***The Grand Prairie in Dansing, South Dakota, a John Dormeier property.*** Then the man himself, John "Big Door" Dormeier, strolled across the screen to lean against the logo with a confident smile and swagger to match. The music cut off, lights came up, and the crowd of about one hundred twenty sat there staring, awestruck.

Before they could rally, black velvet was lifted from easels standing around the perimeter of the stage, each easel showing floor plans, conceptual building sites, color swatches, and design features. A small table featured a table setting for two and a menu she'd lifted from a famous four-star restaurant—only the name at the top had been changed. *Who would know?*

She spoke smoothly, enthusiastically, with a controlled and excited passion about what the economic impact of a five-star resort would mean to the region. After her spiel, she wrapped up with, "And now, to answer all your questions, the man with the vision to foresee all of this, Mr. John Dormeier!"

That did it. The crowd woke up and started applauding—even the two blond reporters with matching hair and dresses seemed caught up in the moment, clapping away and forgetting their professional objectivity.

Three men appeared. A man with sunglasses, dressed in black—obviously some sort of bodyguard, he had sat next to Reese in the limo and ignored everybody. Reese came second, flashy looking, kinda looked like maybe he could be famous if you thought about it for a little. He looked at Estelle and grinned as he walked in. She looked away quickly and suppressed a shudder. Of course, between them and physically towering over them was the third man and the reason everybody was there. The Big Door stepped forward to the podium and crouched over it, bending the mic stand as high as it would go—the crowd laughed appreciatively. And then the questions and answers began.

Why Dansing? Because he hunted pheasants there a few years ago and was haunted by its beauty.

Why a lodge and casino? Because all of his friends liked to do that, and he couldn't wait to invite them out.

Where? It could be anywhere. Meetings with agents and property owners would begin in the spring.

How soon? The sooner the better.

How much? A coy answer, but millions would be needed to realize the scope of his dream.

Millions.

Everyone in the room with property was wondering how to get a few minutes alone with the Big Door or his people. Millions! Finally a buyer had appeared for unwanted property that people had been trying to unload for years, and it didn't seem to matter where the property was. Gears were busily spinning inside every head, thinking about ranches, homes, abandoned buildings that might be sold if-

No, wait! Did you hear him talk about his friends? Better keep it for awhile and wait for top dollar.
People were sitting around, grinning foolishly at each other like they'd just struck oil.

Millions.

*****

Doris knew she was probably going to be trouble but hired the girl anyway. She needed help bussing tables, and this kid sure had the sand anyway. Doris's café had been built on two known quantities that applied to all of humanity: people like to eat, and people like to talk, and her place specialized in both.

The food was serviceable—big portions of ordinary food grown in the Midwest. Scalloped potatoes and ham on Monday, roast beef on Tuesday, chicken potpie on Wednesday, lasagna on Thursday, and fish fillet on Friday. Plus, every day, diners could get pancakes or eggs or hamburgers or fries or mashed potatoes or hash browns. Vegetables were canned corn and canned peas. Occasionally someone would order a salad—that person would get a surprised look and a wedge of lettuce with a bottle of thousand island.

Doris opened at five thirty in the morning with the railroad crowd. The food was good and served fast, including caramel rolls as big as an outstretched hand. Next, the ranchers would come in for the dice games and coffee, then the other regulars building up to lunch, pie, and ice cream, then close at two o'clock sharp, seven days a week.

Then the whole place was cleaned from top to bottom. Doris would prepare what she needed for the next day, lock up, and be out by four. Every August she took the whole month off and went on vacation somewhere exotic. That year was going to be Hawaii, and she carefully divided the number of meals she served by the estimated cost of the trip. This would appear as a line item on each ticket for the entire year. This year it read, "Hawaii, 23 cents."

She was not rich by any stretch, but she was happy. She liked to feed people, and she liked to cook. She also had a soft spot, which she tried to cover up, but it was there anyway.

The young woman she was talking to was, whether she knew it or not, standing right on Doris's soft spot and making it ache. She was so thin! Painfully thin, and when she got off the bus, asking if Doris was hiring, she had a hunted look in her eyes that meant trouble, trouble, trouble.

Too late to hide the Help Wanted sign in the window, so she shrugged. The girl said she could cook and work, and Doris believed it because her hands were calloused and she had that no-nonsense look that capable people have. She told the girl the wage, adding, "This is a small town. A dime is considered a big tip by some of these people." The girl shrugged and asked if she could be paid in cash once a week, which made Doris absolutely certain she was trouble and positively certain she would be gone in a few days.

She folded her arms across her thick chest. "What's your name?"

The girls closed the deal by evading the answer. "You can call me Claire."

Chapter 8 - Hal From-the-Gazette

Hal was impressed. He had never seen a presentation that elaborate. Usually any press conference he was invited to involved a few blueprints or maybe a packet of information handed around. That one was definitely top shelf. The woman with the artsy triangle glasses did a heckava job, and for a while he felt the pride South Dakotans seldom feel.

It *was* a beautiful place, South Dakota was. He'd thought so when he first moved here out of college. Hal was from Connecticut, an Ivy Leaguer who had the talent and connections to be anywhere, but there he was. When pressed about why, he found the answer hard to explain. At first, he'd simply had curiosity and a soft spot for western movies. But then it changed. Most other states boasted about their status, the Don't Mess with Texas bravado. But not here. In every circumstance, when people found out where he was from they asked, "What are you doing *here*?" genuinely puzzled. This hard-bitten humility, driven home by years of economic decay and brutal weather, was coupled with a toughness that got underneath his skin and made him swell with pride when he saw the scenery roll across that screen. *Was that Sam Elliot's voice?* Hal had seen clouds just like those on many mornings, the kind they put on travel posters.

And then his inner cynic tripped him up. *Why such a big deal?* The luster started to fade the more he thought about it. Even though his thirty-five years in journalism had been spent mainly in and around Dansing, he could recognize a fix when he saw one. *Too nice. Too perfect. Too much like a dream come true for a town that was dying. And far too expensive.*

He gave a small sigh. At any rate, he was not going to be the one to ruin anybody's dreams—not because he was against ruining dreams per se. Mainly because he did not want to be the bearer of bad news—the guy they hated for uncovering the truth. He had a lot of friends in town, and the fact of the matter was he *liked* it there. *Nope.* Things looked fishy for sure, but he was not going to be the one to ask the obvious questions. Besides... maybe—just maybe—it might happen. That Ted Turner was buying up a lot of land in the Dakotas. *Maybe this is the same kind of deal.* He was mulling over what angle to use for the story when he saw Stan, the small, intense, reporter who worked at the radio station, stand up.

Oh no. Hal tried to catch his eye. *Sit down, Stan.* If it was a scam, it would unravel eventually. No need to say something stupid. He sighed again. He didn't really know Stan that well. *If he wants to get the whole town pissed at him, I guess he can have at it. At least it would be interesting.*

Chapter 9 - Stan

One of the TV casters—he couldn't tell them apart
—was finishing up a real softball, something about what
he thought about South Dakota, and Dormeier was laying
it on thick—the sweeping plains, the grandeur, the whole
bit. *The guy was huge*. Large hands lapped over the edge
of the podium, the podium itself seemed undersized and
frail, like Dormeier could lift it like a shoe box.

Stan had been standing politely, waiting for his
chance. He glanced over at Hal From-the-Gazette, who
was frowning at him. He knew what the frown was about.
When Stan had started in Dansing about two years before,
he did a story about the fire chief renting out apartments
with no smoke detectors.

Hal had pulled him aside after the story ran on the
morning news and said, "Hey, great story—and I mean
that—but listen: now you'll never get *any* news from the

fire chief. Ever. This town is too small to piss off. Big news is too big. Keep the news small. Missing dogs. Vandalism. School board and city council meetings. Maybe a crime after the arrest is made. Otherwise, you'll kill your sources, understand?"

While he had explained it to Stan, he'd had the same frown on his face.

Stan looked away and felt a small stubborn anger, a contrariness that made his teeth clench a little. Maybe it was because he was hung over. Maybe it was because he was ashamed of himself. More likely it was because Stan just could not help himself. Obvious questions just had to be asked. *They had to be.*

"Excuse me, Mr. Dormeier?"

The Big Door hunched over the podium, giving him a lopsided smile and a raised eyebrow.

"Does this make fiscal sense?"

Most of the crowd had heard about Stan's morning by now—it was, after all, a small town. His question seemed to puzzle them.

Dormeier seemed puzzled too. "Whaddaya mean?"

Stan laid it out. "We are two hours from the nearest interstate. The nearest airports to handle even small commercial are Sioux Falls, Pierre, and Rapid City—all hundreds of miles away. The only gaming casinos that seem to do well nationwide are near population centers—we are not. And although hunting is a good revenue stream, it is only seasonal. Does this make fiscal sense?"

Expressions around him changed throughout his question. The dizzy looks of euphoria right after the media presentation were replaced with bemused humor, then quizzical glances, and then open hostility.

Dormeier's expression had changed too. His eyes focused in on Stan, standing downhill and about fifteen feet away. People sitting next to Stan unconsciously leaned away from him.

"Who are you?" Dormeier said it softly, but the menace was clear. A man sitting next to Stan actually shifted over one seat.

"Stanley Martin, KDAN 870"

The woman with the glasses leaned over a little toward Dormeier, murmuring.

"You're a *radio* reporter?"

Stan said nothing, holding his gaze.

"So Radio Man, you own a business? You a businessman?"

"No, I am not."

"You a millionaire?" This drew snickers from a few.

Stan could feel the bottom of his right foot was wet, from where the cracked sole had leaked melted snow.

"No, I am not."

"Well, Radio Man, I am *both*. So you know what that means?"

Stan knew better, but he could not have held back if he wanted to. "Yes, Mr. Dormeier, it means you have evaded my question by attacking me personally. Please explain why it makes fiscal sense to build a multi-million-dollar resort in Dansing."

John Dormeier's voice became soft again, and a small and dangerous smile appeared. "Little man, I'd like to talk to you sometime—tell you some things—about respect. Respect is important." The man with the sunglasses was suddenly at Dormeier's elbow.

The room was quiet for a full two seconds, every eye focused on the scene, before the woman with the eyeglasses cut in. "Such it is and has always been with visionary people—people laughed at Edison's light bulb, at the Wright Brothers—and skeptics will always question what they cannot see." She went on for a while, defusing the tension, diverting the attention away. The press conference ended with the woman telling those gathered that the Dormeier Team would meet with prospective property sellers and investors in a nearby hotel suite throughout the remainder of the day, and a small group rushed to sign up for a time on a nearby clipboard, but others stayed in small knots to comment on the question and speculate on why Dansing? The buzzing voices grew louder as people argued both sides of the issue.

Stan was alone in the crowd with the vague but real sensation that he had stepped over some line. He was suddenly very tired. Now that the presentation was over, large mercury lights were buzzing overhead, bathing the room in stark, mechanical light. Stan was tired, and his right foot was wet. And he was hungry. He couldn't do much about the other things, but maybe he would feel better if he ate something. Maybe he should get some breakfast.

******

*"You look like hell, McGarvey. Didn't you sleep?"
Stan shook his head. High strung, unhappy. The military
was not what they said it might be. Out of college with a
degree in history and literature, Stan was doomed to either
teach or try another major. He had tried teaching, thinking
maybe he could coach, but track coaches were not needed
and only tolerated for those who could teach something,
anything, and he had no ability in that line. It was an army
recruiter who had talked about the glory of sport and the
privilege of serving his country competing in armed forces
track meets. The recruiter had not mentioned that between
occasional track meets was senseless drilling, thick-
headed officers, and for those who didn't say "yes, sir"
right away, guard duty and KP. He could not relax. He felt
trapped in a very large machine that made no sense. The
irregular hours of guard duty made insomnia worse.*

*The question came from a corporal from West
Virginia, a freckled man named Burke with a hollow leg,
who saw him lying in his bunk, red eyed. "C'mon, let's get
a couple shots at the club. That'll quiet your mind." Stan
hesitated; he did not care for the taste of alcohol, and
memories of a father who drank soured him. "Does that
work?"*

Burke laughed. "Every night!"

Chapter 10 - Estelle

She wanted out. Those guys were nuts—especially Reese. He kept fidgeting, shifting his shoulders and arms like he was trying on a suit, and combing his hair. After that he'd look around grinning to see if anyone had noticed. His taste in clothes was on the loud side, and the looks he gave her made her skin crawl.

The other guy in the dark glasses—Robinson, they called him—was almost worse: no expression, probably some sort of ex-Special Forces dude that could kill with a paper clip. She had worked for years in PR and had gotten used to strange clients with half truths, but the Three Stooges were a piece of work. She tried to keep a calm façade while Dormeier went on his rant, pounding the limo's armrest until it broke.

"Who *is* that guy? That little son of a bitch is gonna ruin everything! Didja hear him? Didja *hear* him?"

Now she knew there was some sort of scam going on. She tried to smooth it over. "You'll always get critics in the press. Everybody expects it, and nobody listens to them. It's nothing."

Dormeier glared at her. He wanted to hit her—she could tell. No wonder that poor wife of his looked like the walking dead. *I'd drink too with that Neanderthal stomping around.* The advice she'd given was good—overreacting to unfavorable press often made things worse, but she was done giving advice to that moron. *Shut up and look for a way out.*

Robinson was the one who finally said something. "She's probably right. In any case, just use what you have to get what you want."

Dormeier looked at him. "Like what?"

Robinson shrugged. "Money."

Dormeier then looked at her.

She shifted a little, uncomfortable under his gaze. *Why did I take this job?* Then she nodded. "Yes, stories can go away with money being spent—or *not being spent*—in the right way."

Dormeier said nothing, waiting for her to continue.

She sighed inwardly. Then, with Dormeier glowering, Reese leering, and the Special Forces dude just... *looking*, she penciled out a strategy that would bury the reporter in money.

*****

Greta was eighteen at the end of the war—just another victim of the führer's vision of a third reich. Her

*mother had been killed first, in an air raid. Her brother
was killed next, somewhere on the western front. Her
father remarried shortly after that happened, but then he
was killed too, before the fall of Berlin. The Americans
came, and at least food became more plentiful. She found a
job serving meals to American soldiers; she kept her head
down and wore loose clothing—all men were the same no
matter what uniform they wore.*

*A new government was set up and with it a new
monetary system—every German was to be given fifty
marks. One night after working her shift her stepmother
met her at the door with a suitcase of her belongings and
her money. "Take them and go." Before she could react,
the door was closed in her face, and she was alone.*

*It might have been something to cry about, but she
had never cared for the woman, and there seemed no more
room for tears after all the suffering.*

*She took the streetcar back to work because that
was the only thing she could think of to do. The officers'
club was closed. She sat on her suitcase underneath a
street lamp for an unknown period of time.*

*She was still sitting there when she saw Jimmy for
the first time.*

*He was tall and lean, with a prominent jaw and
eyes as serene as summer.*

*"Hello, Fräulein." His American accent was thick
as molasses, his dress uniform a little short at the cuffs. He
was a private, about the millionth American who had tried
to make a play for her.*

*There under the street light he got down on one
knee and looked her in the eye. His face was without guile*

or pretense, and when she looked in his eyes, she knew right then she was gone.

"I been watchin' you, Fräulein, from over across the street. And I believe with all my heart that you are the one for me."

It was not that easy, but it was that certain, and nineteen months later, she was with him in South Dakota, near a small town called Dansing, a newly minted war bride and US citizen.

She never looked back. Jimmy was what he was, a product of sunshine and wind; he had an easy carefree manner and was always kind, his touch a healing balm to her war-sick soul.

He taught her the ways of living in the strange land. Taught her to shoot and cook what they shot. Their land was a patch of prairie indistinguishable from the countless other miles of prairie, but it was theirs. They were on the outskirts of town, the way Jimmy liked it, and together they built a small house.

She was eight months pregnant when the roof was finished, and as Jimmy was coming down the ladder, he slipped and fell wrong, broke his neck, and died. She lost the baby right then too. Grief or shock or whatever.

The sheriff and a man from town came out to help her move back home, they said.

"Get the hell off our land," was what she said back. They were taken aback and did not know what to do. She went and got the big Mauser Jimmy had brought back from Germany, a sniper rifle. He had taught her never to point it unless she meant business, and that day she surely did. "I said get the hell off our land."

They said they'd come back, but they never did. They said she'd leave, but she never did either. She stayed there alone with her grief and her memories.

That was, my God, how long ago?

Jimmy and the baby were buried in the back by some lilacs she planted. She talked to Jimmy every day— he was still her strength and companion.

It was Jimmy that helped her fight to get his small inheritance from some money-grubbing cousins, it was Jimmy that gave her the courage to get a job in town for a time working as a waitress, and it was Jimmy and her who decided it was a good idea to lease some land to the radio station for a tower they wanted built.

Now the radio station was another companion, sign-on to sign-off, the signal so powerful you could sometimes hear the radio coming off a bread pan in the kitchen.

She had news and weather farm prices during the day and ball games and the stars at night. And Jimmy.

She was the size of a gray-haired boy and about worn out. Yet Jimmy told her to wait and be patient. There were maybe one or two things left to do, and when they were done, they would be together.

Chapter 11 - Claire

Claire glanced out the café window at the weather —a habit one developed early in life on the plains.

Everything looked as though it had all changed— again. This time the wind had slipped back a few notches, the frayed flag flying over the post office (all flags in South Dakota are frayed—they last about two months before beating themselves to death) was rippling gently about ten miles an hour, and the sun was out. Puddles had already started forming in the street, and by midafternoon, the snow would be melted. The talk around her was weather talk—it always was. This time a rancher was holding a mug of coffee, shaking dice, and telling other ranchers how certain he was about an early spring thaw. A few hours before, the morning rush had talked about a blizzard. That was how fast weather changed.

The bell over the door rang, and she saw Stan slip in to his usual spot, coming in after a couple of ranchers, the way he always did. She spotted him right away and hid a smile. She wasn't sure why he didn't like opening the door himself. Maybe he didn't like the attention the bell drew when the door hit it. He was a peculiar man—different from what she was used to seeing but in an appealing kind of way. He was not a big man, nor well dressed or outgoing.

He had a kind of compressed quality, which some people with a lot of energy had, and a rare, direct gaze like a flash of light reflected off a lake or ocean. She resisted the temptation to brush the hair behind her ear but could not resist smoothing her apron.

Silly.

No man she had ever known had been anything but trouble. The last one had tried to kill her. He'd been nice enough to marry but, after the vows, started showing a mean side. That was ten years before—she still had a small scar above her right eyebrow… and more than a few more inside.

Men were trouble.

But still.

He slipped onto a stool at the end of the counter by the pie safe. He was poor, anyone could see that, with frayed cuffs and collar and a wrinkled tie. He counted his money carefully, as though he knew how little he had but was recounting it to make sure. She wasn't sure, but she felt he hadn't always been poor. He caught her watching, and their eyes met before he quickly glanced away. He

kind of reminded her of a stray dog she'd found as a kid—
skinny, run down, with bottomless eyes.

She held up a glass carafe. "Coffee?"

He nodded. She knew his name. They lived in
Dansing after all, and "the fella from the radio" was a
popular topic. Whenever he left, there was plenty to be
talked about, because he was Not From Here.

And he must have known her name, at least the
name she went by, because it was on her name tag and
because it was shouted about every three minutes during
the rush. But they had never introduced themselves, so
they continued an anonymous dance that would not
amount to anything.

She poured the last of the coffee into a mug,
slipped it onto the worn countertop in front of him, turned,
and set up the Bunn for another pot. A dog-eared menu
was in front of him, but they both knew what he would
order. The cheapest thing on the menu was the biscuits and
gravy—a buck eighty. Truth was, she was aching to feed
him as much as he could hold, but that would not do—he
never had more than a few dollars.

"I think I will have the biscuits and gravy please,"
he said after a bit. His voice was deep and resonant, a
voice that did not fit the skin and bones of his frame but
somehow did fit those eyes, blue and sometimes grey—
today bloodshot.

Men are Trouble.

But like a moth to a flame, she seemed drawn to
this one.

She tried something. Casually, she put three
biscuits on his plate instead of two and ladled on too much

sausage gravy. In a noncommittal voice she stated that the breakfast rush was over and since lunchtime was coming on, she didn't want to have to throw the gravy away.

He paused and looked at the heaping plate suspiciously. She looked at him guilelessly.

"Well… how much would this be?"

Off-handedly, she said, "The same price—no difference." The damn starving fool was pondering his pride while she pretended not to notice.

His voice was still formal, like a business agreement. "Very well, then."

He set a paper napkin on his lap and, with impeccably neat movements and manners, started eating, quickly and efficiently.

That was the best part. Being a waitress was tough and menial, and the tips were small and the hours long and the feet tired. But she found satisfaction, great satisfaction, in watching a hungry man eat.

Especially that man. She had others to tend to but not a lot. She gave him his space, bringing him fresh coffee when his mug was empty, tending him carefully like that stray dog from her youth.

The plate was empty, wiped clean. With careful movements he wiped the counter clean of nonexistent spills and set his mug on the plate with the flatware and the napkin on top. He stood and said formally, "Thank you. It was delicious."

"You're more than welcome." Again she fought the ridiculous urge to sweep some hair behind her ear.

Then he slipped out. That time with a truck driver.

Next to his plate there was a small pile of coins. She did not have to count it to know that it would be twenty percent of the tab.

Chapter 12 - Reese

All Reese knew was this was supposed to be fun, but it was not. He came with on a lark. He'd liked westerns as a kid and thought it might be like a movie. He felt stupid, having thought there might be cowboys and Indians and school marms and whorehouses. But all this town was (what was the name of it again?) was just cold and windy and flat and boring. He combed his hair again, flexed his shoulders, and flashed a grin. He had a lot of grins, and he practiced them throughout his day. The current one was the "don't mess with me" grin. He wasn't doing it for anyone but himself, but the PR chick with the glasses must've thought it was for her, and she looked nervous. She had just given them some ideas about getting rid of the radio guy, and a lot of them made sense. She looked good—if you liked that artsy, corporate type. Maybe he could have some fun.

The two of them had been told to find a realtor office and book some properties to view, but the realtor was gone, and the office was unlocked, dusty, and cold, and he was bored, bored, bored.

"Hey," he said, standing closer.

She looked scared, so he used another grin that suggested she should be. Again, not his type, but it might be kinda fun to see what she looked like if she was more respectful.

"How come you don't like me?" he asked, too close. He blew on her face and grinned. Behind the glare and blank face he could see a flash of fear in her eyes. That was better. She was probably a fighter, but that was okay too.

The door opened behind him with a rattle and a gust of cold wind.

"Hey there, folks! I'm Clyde Rheems. How can I be of service today?" He was out of breath, and his gold realtor jacket had some folds in it as though it didn't get worn much.

"I'll be right back." She was smart, too. Taking advantage of the interruption, she whisked right out the door, past the realtor, and got into the limo. The driver wasn't there, but the keys were. A moment later, it revved down the street as though she had no intention of coming back, which she didn't.

She did not answer any more phone calls or collect the remainder of her fee. Dormeier got pissed, of course, but Reese stuck with his smile and his story until it blew over. After all, there were a lot more important things to be done in the next few days.

Chapter 13 - Robinson

Robinson was concerned but not too concerned. Reese was not a professional, and that was what the problem was. He would do stuff that was dangerous. Scare people. Push them around. Yes, that was a necessary part of getting things done, but one did it because one *needed* to do it, not because one wanted to.

He sighed. Maybe he should quit. *This job may be the riskiest one yet.* But the money was good. Really good. His first job out of reform school had featured lousy pay and crummy benefits, with one notable exception—Uncle Sam paid for the training. And being young and angry and gung ho, he took all of it: combat experience, hand-to-hand, marksmanship, jumping out of anything that moved, special ops. Some things he was better at than others, but he was good at all of it.

He could have been career, *should* have been career, but rules of engagement said they had been a little overzealous after a firefight. *Like they knew anything about what fighting was really like.* He avoided Leavenworth with a dishonorable discharge and tried his skills elsewhere. He tried paramilitary for a while but didn't trust the men he fought with. He then tried personal security—that paid better but was pretty boring. He found out he had become addicted to the adrenaline, to the edges of chaos.

Then he met Dormeier, and right then he knew that this was his ticket. Dormeier was rich and probably unscrupulous—most definitely unscrupulous—but Robinson did not care to know any details. And there was the added benefit of no team, no chance for a weak link—just him as the personal army of the Big Door. Much easier that way. Safer too.

Dormeier paid a very nice salary, which Robinson lived off of, and a much nicer bonus that consisted of under-the-table cash, untaxed and immediately deposited in an account in the Cayman Islands. By the time Robinson tired of the adrenaline, he would literally sail off into the sunset of some Caribbean island. That was why he was here. Reese was a punk—an undisciplined punk with a dangerous streak but no different from some others he had dealt with.

He could handle the next few days. He had done tougher things.

Chapter 14 - Dansing

The problem with Dansing was a problem that had been evident in almost every South Dakota town for the past forty years. It was dying. That was no one's fault, really. It was just a hard place to live. This was not immediately evident in the early days. Settlers poured across the landscape, grabbing land up left and right— starting at the Alleghenies and moving on west. They'd put the sod to the plow and plant it, using the same methods their fathers taught them. Those methods had in turn been passed down from their father's fathers, all the way back to the European continent. Plow it black. Keep it tilled. Plant in the spring. Harvest in the fall. Tried and true, every one of them—that was until these methods ran into the great American plains.

Of course no one knew it was doomed right away. Huge land rushes were announced by the federal government on a regular basis, fueled by the railroads and by land-starved immigrants. And the land was perfect! Flat as a table, rich and lush, not a rock on it. Weather experts proclaimed the scientific truth that once you broke that sod to the plow the rains would follow. For a few years that was true—bumper crops, land booms, and prosperity. And the farmers were too naïve to know that a "weather expert" was an oxymoron.

The plentiful rains were part of a rare wet cycle. When they stopped, everything dried up: the crops and the income that came with it, the grocery stores and the implement dealers, the car dealers, the clothing shops, and the movie theaters. All of it dried up and started blowing away. Then the towns started dying. No one wanted to admit it, naturally. Prairie fires, grasshoppers, hail, tornadoes... *I mean it couldn't be bad every year. Why, just wait 'til next year!*

With every bad event that seemed to happen annually, kids grew up, went off to school, and found that life was a lot easier somewhere else. Farms that were one hundred sixty acres were bought up and merged into bigger outfits that required fewer and fewer people, so the towns started merging their schools together—once, then twice—then the whole works would be closed down when there weren't enough taxes or kids to make a go of it.

Now with the railroads mostly gone, most towns clung to one of the two interstates that crossed the state as the only chance for commerce, and Dansing was a long way from either.
County historians knew that Dansing itself had been a bribe. The town fathers offered to name the town (even the

county!) after a railroad executive named Frederick Dansing if he would put the line through. It worked, and the next town over copied their success by calling their town Frederick.

Frederick Dansing died in the early 1920s, and his namesakes were close on his heels.
Frederick, South Dakota, was currently an unincorporated group of buildings: two bars, one church, a feedlot, and an abandoned elevator next to a discontinued rail spur, and only Dansing was left.

In fact, in all of Dansing County, only eleven hundred souls were left. Those mostly friendly, stubborn souls went to church on Sunday, rooted for the nine-man football team (unfortunately named the Prancers) on Friday, and went about their business the other days, pretending they were not doomed.

Doomed, that was, until the basketball star from out east came to talk about his dreams. Dreams that made people wonder. Maybe. *Maybe things might change a little*.
Stranger things had happened.

Chapter 15 - Dormeier

The Big Door was settling down. He hated being talked back to by anybody, much less a scruffy two-bit reporter. He had been *this* close to—well anyway, that was done. The woman from the PR firm was right. He had spent about forty-five minutes after the press conference working over the plan she had laid out in the limo. Then he reentered the convention hall and circulated among those still gathered.

As he talked to different groups, he dropped a series of messages; maybe he had been wrong about the reception of the community toward his vision; how could a radio station squelch the dreams of an entire town? *I mean this is a business-driven town, isn't it?* Why would businesses support a radio station that was anti-business? Grim faces among that small knot of people proved that his words hit the mark.

Next he needed to work on the Big Thing for that night. He looked at his two employees, taking inventory.

Robinson was proving to be more versatile. He seemed to be able to read people and see what their weaknesses might be. Reese was... well, Reese. He had always been a loose cannon, but he was still a cannon. If he needed somebody to be intimidated or maybe something more, Bobby Reese was happy to oblige, and he was all in on helping tonight. So that was what it was.

"Bobby, tell me again what happened this afternoon?"

Reese shrugged one shoulder at a time, tweaked his neck, and grinned. "I dunno. She just freaked and left. Said she was tired of waiting and that her job was done, and she just bolted."

"And took the limo?"

"Yeah, said she was gonna come back, but I got a feeling she ain't."

Dormeier stared at Bobby while he went through a series of shrugs and twitches. Geez, no wonder she'd freaked. He sighed. She was right about her job anyway— he was pretty much done with her now. *Good luck getting paid. Screw her.*

He sighed again and looked at Robinson

"Okay, just a little while longer. Robinson, I know it's not what you're used to, but you and Bobby together are gonna need to talk with this realtor guy. Book as many appointments as you can for, say... the next three weeks. I wanna make sure that anyone who has money or property in this county has an opportunity to book a time to show what they have, got it? As far as anyone knows, we are scouting properties through the first part of June and planning on breaking ground in the fall."

Both men nodded.

"And I'm gonna go over to the hotel again and make sure everybody who is anybody gets invited to the party. Be good." He looked hard at Reese. "You understand?"

Bobby flexed his shoulders and grinned.

Chapter 16 - Happy Jack

Happy Jack was not happy. He sat in his office with the phone off the hook and stuck in a file drawer. He had the monitor turned up, listening to the station, but gave up after a while. He absolutely hated listening to Larry Karl puke all over the airwaves. He thought about tuning in to a good station but reluctantly decided that was disloyal. The lights were off, but that was no good either— the girls knew he was in. They kept sliding notes under the door with obvious glee. He massaged his sweating forehead and tried to rub his headache away.

The press conference had been that morning, and as the day progressed, the news got worse. The Big Door and the twitchy grinning guy with the comb—what was his name, Billy? Bubba?—had been talking to business owners throughout town about possible land deals and loudly worrying about the negative response they were feeling from the local media. Those same businesses were advertisers on KDAN and knew the power of pressure. They were quickly becoming ex-advertisers. The phone calls that day had all been the same:

"Helluva deal, Jack! We got the best thing that ever happened to this town, and your fella has to shoot his mouth off. I don't like *it*, and I don't like *him*, and I don't like to put my good name anywhere near it. Until he's gone, pull my ads."

Hiding was not working. Two hours before, two salespeople had read him the riot act about lost sales and commissions. The commercial log had been printed the day before, and that day it was full of ink where ads had been crossed off. The bitch of it was, Stan Martin was the best radio voice and the best reporter he had ever hired. Happy Jack had counted himself lucky to get him a few years before, drinking aside. While he was thinking, he heard a knock at the door, and three more slips of paper slipped under.

Oh jeez.

Chapter 17 - Larry

Larry was having a high old time. He'd wrangled
a part-timer into running his shift so he could go to the
press conference and had found the perfect spot, standing
right behind that Sioux Falls news gal. He was able to
sneak quite a few peeks down her blouse and still catch
Stan going up against The Big Door.

It was awesome.

Presently, he was back at the station, pulling his
shift in his usual fashion, smoking cigarettes and holding
court on the ratty couch in the front lobby. There, reclining
on the Naugahyde, he would smoke a cigarette and gossip
with the girls about whatever, one ear tuned to the on-air
monitor over the couch. Then, with seconds left in a spot
or song, he would leap to his feet and bound into the
studio, clicking on the mic with one hand and reporting the
time and temp while he fished for a cart or record with his

other. Those who heard him on the radio would have had a much higher opinion of him if they actually saw how he worked.

"K-D-A-N, fourteen minutes before the top of the hour and thirty-four degrees in the metro." He liked to say "in the metro" instead of "in town" because to his finely tuned ear it sounded better, even though the nearest metropolitan area was probably Denver.

There were brief pauses in his delivery as he grabbed for an album. It was a Dolly Parton album, and he told one of his favorite jokes. "This is off of Dolly Parton's greatest tits album." *Funny.* Then, before Dolly could begin to complain about working nine to five, Larry was back in the lobby, slouching on the couch. "Didja hear that? Greatest tits... Get it?" He easily spent fifty minutes of every hour, sometimes in fifteen-second increments, lying flat on that couch and smoking. Achieving such a high level of laziness was an art form, and Larry Karl was a master.

That day was a rare one, the girls and he were in fine fettle, hashing and re-hashing the whole press conference, wondering with glee just how much trouble Stan was in.

Of course Stan was right—something was fishy about the whole thing—but if a rich gabillionaire wanted to set up a resort here, why not? *And the women!* He could imagine all the women that would tag along looking for all the rich friends of Dormeier. "Too bad about ol' Stanley, though," he said out loud, not meaning it at all. "They are going to bounce his ass hard." After his shift, he spent the rest of the afternoon not working and lounging around the office, gossiping about if and when Happy Jack would drop the axe.

Chapter 18 - Stan

Stan sat in Happy Jack's office, staring at a point on Jack's forehead while the axe was being dropped. A bead of sweat was forming above the manager's left eyebrow, and Stan wondered if it would materialize into a trickle before Jack was finished with his speech.

Jack was perched on the edge of his desk, arms folded, lips pursed. Stan had been witness to many of Jack's poses in the past—behind the desk, seated, with fingertips steepled together or leaning against a window frame, rays of light cut in stripes by the venetian blinds playing across his stern features—but it looked like he had finally settled on the benevolent-yet-wronged employer on the edge of his desk as the best option.

South Dakota is a right-to-work state, so Happy Jack could have fired Stan for any reason at all but had decided on "broadcasting under the influence." Stan had to admit it was neater that way, not having to mention the pile of cancelled ad contracts stacked in Happy Jack's in tray, and the whole slippery slope of the caving-under-financial-pressure thing.

Stan stayed calm—detached, really. He deserved it. His only regret was that he knew he was not being fired for being drunk but for doing about the only decent bit of reporting he had done the whole time he was there.

Oh well. He was not really worried about money. The truth was he could work at a fast-food place and make more money and have better hours, a fact the jocks brought up several times a week. No, he figured he would have a few days to rest and think about his options outside of radio. Maybe now he could get some sleep.

Maybe I should get a drink.

Chapter 19 - Dormeier

He came back to the hotel room. They called it a suite because it was the biggest and nicest room in the hotel and therefore the town, but it was two steps away from dingy, a few years away from outdated, and smack dab in the middle of blandly sterile. But it did have a fully stocked minifridge, and Marie was halfway through its contents as he let himself in.

She was a good drinker. She could hold her own with many people larger than her, and she did not get maudlin or weepy. On the contrary, she got brighter, edgier, more alive. Her usually listless eyes got sharper and glinted steel. Her tall, thin frame became more supple and fluid, her gestures less timid and more direct.

In fact, he had first seen her when she was half in the bag, at one of her father's charity events, and what initially attracted him was her direct gaze and bold movements.

She was bold now as he closed the door, tossing back the last of something clear, gin maybe.

"You are a son of a bitch, John."

It was a tired old game they'd started years before. She would goad him, and he would react. He backhanded her with a slap, almost without thought or malice even.

She fell the way she always did, loose and detached, onto an ugly green couch, a small welt already showing next to her lip, eyes sharp and alive. *That was stupid*. People might ask about how she got that mark.

"Why did you bring me here?" Her gesture took in the room and its tired contents.
He shrugged, not sure if she would believe him and not sure that he cared. "Fresh air."

She laughed suddenly with genuine mirth. She had serious allergies, something they both knew, and it was quite possible to believe he had driven to a place loaded with pollen just to see her suffer.

Her laugh and smile died away, and her eyes grew wary as she studied him. "So what happens now?"

He turned, walked to the minifridge, grabbed a beer, and twisted off the cap. "Not much. Just a thing at the hotel bar tonight. A dog-and-pony show for investors. Probably better if you don't come."

"What if I want to?"

"I told people you weren't feeling well, so you better stay here."

"Did you tell Robinson that?"

"Yeah."

"So that means I will definitely not be leaving here, huh?"

"Guess not."

She looked at him steadily, saying nothing. He looked away. *Stupid to even have come up here.* He liked violence, was comfortable with it in the heat of the moment, but this planned, cold violence done quietly so it would look like an accident, that was not who he was. Finally he tossed back the beer in one long swallow and went for the door.

As he opened it, he caught her eyes looking at him in the reflection of the mirrored tiles by the doorframe. Her smile was sour, and her eyes were bright with tears. "Good-bye John."

Chapter 20 - Stan

Stan had learned by now that all transient people got screwed. Every time he moved he had to get a different phone number, which meant paying an additional hook-up charge. This also applied to utilities, driver's license, license plates, and especially rent. Every placed he had lived required two months' rent due before move-in. The extra money was theoretically the deposit you got back once you moved out unless you had damaged the apartment. This was a tired farce, for who is to say what damages are? Was a twenty-year-old faucet that started leaking in the last three months really damage? How much damage did a stain do on a threadbare carpet riddled with preexisting stains?

Stan had an appointment with the landlady for eleven in the morning.

It was Dansing, so of course she knew he'd been fired. She was probably one of the people who'd complained to Happy Jack. She had a number of run-down places throughout town she would love to unload for the good of the community and at enormous profit.

Tomorrow was the beginning of a new month, and he needed to act fast before another month's rent was tacked on. If he was on his best behavior, maybe she would take pity on him and give him back his deposit.

****

Stan had a voice for radio, but he looked okay for TV. He had a good jaw line and eyes that were... interesting.

It shouldn't have made any difference since his job was news, but of course it did. People prefer to get news from people that look good. Out of the military, he had gotten a job in radio at a TV/radio combo in Raleigh. He worked nights and weekends, reading the news and pulling a shift on the AC station. Turnover was high, and every time someone left, the stations did a two-month nationwide search to find "the best talent out there," but every time they wound up promoting someone in-house instead. Oh well.

He was young and single and didn't have a life, so he was offered and took a weekend gig doing the early-evening news for the TV side. He didn't care for it—he didn't like the voices shouting at him through his earpiece or the feigned friendliness the station required between the anchors, but they liked him. He probably would have graduated to a network if the insomnia hadn't gotten to him. Drinking didn't work very well, but it worked some. He miscalculated the dosage one Saturday morning and woke up drunk half an hour before the newscast. To make matters worse, it was a summer schedule and because of vacations, he was to carry the whole newscast himself, the weather and sports desk, the news—the whole half hour.

No way he should have been let on the air. Someone should have stepped in, played a "we're having technical difficulties" announcement, and moved on. But the regular news director was on vacation too, and the part-timer didn't know any better. At least three heads rolled after that. The news director got tossed for handling the scheduling poorly, the part-time news director for not running an infomercial or "for God's sake, some cartoons even." And of course Stan.

In the long haul of Stan's career, it was not the only time he was ever drunk at work, but it was the first and most embarrassing time. It ended his television career and started his long, slow trip down the ladder of rated markets, something he called The Fall.

Chapter 21 - Marjorie

Marjorie DeWalt was fifty-five but looked seventy. From the frown lines deeply creasing her face, she looked like a third-world refugee who had faced enormous hardship. That was far from the truth but did not prevent her feeling downtrodden anyway. Somewhere along the line, she'd decided that people—excluding her—were just no damn good. That included her husband, a mild-mannered banker who married her before the frown lines showed up and gave her an instant ticket to upward mobility, a ticket she immediately grabbed and almost as immediately disdained him for.

She owned about thirty rental properties in Dansing and was amazed at the destructive tendencies and larcenous hearts of the people who lived in them.

About three times a week, she would receive some kind of complaint about a leaky roof or broken toilet or faulty heater. Those were called in to her answering machine and promptly ignored.

Eventually tenants would learn to put a bucket under the leak or wear an extra sweater or use the bathroom at the 7-11. What did they expect for the meager rent they paid—the Taj Mahal?

And presently, she had to meet with Stanley Martin, that trouble-making announcer from the radio station. No doubt, he would want some of his deposit back as well.

Having dealt with that kind of people before, Marjorie knew how tenants would hide damage just before an inspection, so many times a month, she would stop by unannounced, when the tenants weren't around to see what she could see. This blatant abuse of privacy was her best way to find damage as it happened and to snoop around in other people's lives, looking for dirt.

Stanley Martin was an alcoholic, something she was delighted to discover. On and about the first and fifteenth of each month—payday, she figured—she would find an empty bottle of vodka in his wastebasket. Cheap stuff. Other than that, he was the perfect tenant. His possessions were limited: a few sets of clothes, a small TV and radio, and one plate and one fork and one saucepan, all three of which were dirty in the sink whenever she happened by. Having a messy kitchen was hard when he had only three kitchen utensils and when his diet consisted of Dinty Moore stew or TV dinners. The oven didn't get dirty, either. In fact, he even seemed to clean the place every week or so. Over the two years he had lived there, the bathroom had become less and less grimy, and once he had even painted, a fact that outraged her in a way she could not quite understand.

She knocked on his door at exactly 11:00a.m., and he opened the door.

"Good morning, Mrs. Dewalt." His manners were perfect, and in truth he was rather handsome for a poor man, but his eyes gave him away. There was a slight world-wise cast to them, a bottomless understanding that he knew who she was and what she would do today.

She stepped into the apartment and covered her unexpected unease with a brusque demeanor. "Yes, well, there's no beating around the bush. No doubt you'll want to break your rental agreement, with no chance of me filling the lease on short notice, I might add, and now you want me to inspect things before you leave."

"Yes, I suppose it's been quite some time since you've been in here." His voice was deep and soft and ever so gently sarcastic.

Infuriating.

The inspection took forty-five minutes. Those things usually took longer, sometimes up to two hours while she gleefully exposed the shocking damage to sheepish tenants, but not that time. Stan had produced a detailed inspection of his own, which he had made at the time of his initial deposit.

She had forgotten about that.

On that neatly folded document was listed all the damages noted at that time, along with her initials estimating when those repairs would be done. None of the repairs had been made. To make matters worse, he had added a clause at the end of the paperwork stating that he could initiate cosmetic repairs—i.e. painting—as long as he didn't change the color of the apartment. She had forgotten that too. And she had forgotten that she signed it.

Her eyes blazed with rage.

"Well, Mr. Martin. I imagine you think you are entitled to a return of your deposit."

"I do."

"Well, I can't say I agree. But as a favor to you and to prove I am on the up and up, I will hire an inspector at my own expense to mediate. If you leave me a forwarding address, I will make sure I send you any deposit due."

He looked at her with eyes that changed slowly to ice. She wanted to look away but found she couldn't.

"Has this ever resulted in a return of deposit in the past?"

She shifted uncomfortably, color rising up her neck to her cheeks. "I can't tell you the exact times, dates, and deposits of every tenant I've had."

His eyes changed again. This time, his features shifted to one of thinly veiled disdain. "I don't think you'll be needing my new address. Good-bye, Mrs. DeWalt." He pointed toward the door.

Her hands were shaking with rage when she got to her car. *Kicked out of my own property!* Her face was clenched in a mask of fury. She kicked the side of her Cadillac and then kicked it again. How dare he call her integrity into question! She gunned out of the parking lot, nearly hitting a kid on a bicycle. *Stupid kid.*

Later, when she cooled down a bit, she dropped the car off at the dealer to have the body shop fix the tiny crescent-shaped dents her high heels had made in the door panel. The bill came to $235, which made her mad all over again.

That had been the amount of Stanley Martin McGarvey's deposit.

Chapter 22 - Stan

Three hundred eleven dollars plus some change…
it made a pathetically small roll of bills in his pocket. He
needed enough to get out of town, enough to get the Shark
fixed, enough to buy some food, and maybe enough to fix
his shoes. He thought about the liquor store downtown but
pushed the thought away. *Not today. Not now.*

First things first. The last day of March was
remarkably pleasant weather-wise; the ever-present wind
was just a soft breeze, and the smell of mud and grass
meant that someday spring would come. And after a long
winter, the sixty-degree sunshine felt almost hot. The
Amoco Station was about half a mile away, and by the
time he got there, a few beads of sweat had collected on
Stan's brow, and he was carrying his coat over one arm.

Crazy weather.

Loren Krens had called him a few days before to tell him the Shark was done, but he did not have the money to pick it up. He was going to wait until Friday, payday, but Happy Jack had had Lorna give him his severance check right away. Two actually. The second came after Stan mentioned to Happy Jack that he had ten vacation days saved up, and after looking at him steadily for a few long moments, Happy Jack suddenly became magnanimous and had Lorna cut the other check for vacation pay.

Loren was in the back of the station by the lift. He was underneath a rusted-out Cutlass, poking at it glumly. All the jocks had their cars serviced at Loren's because he was cheap and softhearted. The Cutlass belonged to Eddie. Eddie's last name was Polish and unpronounceable. His air name was Eddie Dangerous, a ridiculous name that Eddie had come up with himself and in no way described him. He worked from six to one in the morning, the bottom rung of the ladder, so everyone just called him Eddie or "the new guy"—or "the Nug" if he had done something especially stupid. Nug stood for New Useless Guy.

"Lookit this." Loren motioned Stan over to him as though they were continuing a conversation. "One hundred ninety-eight thousand miles on it and doesn't use a drop of oil, but this"—he poked again, and a shower of rust fell —"this cancer is gonna kill it. Too damn bad. These Cutlasses sure are runners."

That was Loren's weakness—he loved every car he saw. He loved Eddie's Cutlass, he loved the peeling green LTD Larry Karl drove, but he especially loved the Shark. The Shark was Stan's car, a 1970 Chrysler 300. It was dark—dull grey, almost black. It'd looked menacing ten years before when Stan first saw it in a used-car lot. He wasn't the type of person who usually named cars, but he called it the Shark before he signed the papers, and The Shark it remained.

Before The Fall, Stan had taken meticulous care of it—or rather had others care for it. He wasn't one for fuzzy dice or that sort of thing, but he kept it sterile on the inside and spotless on the outside. When he had money, he would bring it in monthly, fussing about some small noise. Since the move to Dansing, however, the Shark—like everything else Stan owned—had to just make the best of it. When it started blowing steam a few weeks before, he had no idea what to do but drove it three miles over to Loren's Amoco, something that made Loren quite upset at the time.

"What if you'da overheated it? Cracked the block?" By the time he was done lecturing Stan, Stan felt as though he had been caught beating a small child. Anyway, there it sat, and the time had come to find out how bad the news was.

"Well, I guess you're gonna need the Shark." Everyone called it the Shark, Loren included. The news of Stan's firing was everywhere.

"Yep." Stan didn't really want to talk about it.

Neither did Loren especially. Outside of cars, Loren had few interests. He scratched at his beard, which began somewhere below his neck and ended just underneath his dirt-flecked glasses.

"Blown radiator. And the hoses are pretty mushy. Some of the belts are cracked, and your back tires are gettin' worn. There's some play in your steering that needed fixing, and your rear seal is dripping a tad."

Stan's spirits sank with each diagnosis.

"I know you need to get out of town, but I didn't want you breaking down on the way."

"How much?"

Loren scratched his beard again and shifted a bit.

"Forty dollars."

Stan stared. "Forty dollars?"

Loren looked away as though embarrassed. "Yeah, well, it just took a little solder for the radiator, and I got some coolant from an aluminum block engine that I had to change but should still work in yours. I had a wrecked car with the same size tires that I swapped out..." Loren continued ticking off all the ways he fixed cars on a shoestring.

When he presented the bill the parts added up to fourteen dollars, and the rest was labor. Stan did not know what to say.

"Thanks." The word seemed totally inadequate.

Loren shrugged, scratching his beard again, then he looked at Stan defiantly. "Truth is, I never liked that Dormeier fella on the TV. Thought he played dirty."

Chapter 23 - Reese

Reese found it remarkably easy. All he had to do
was go see the prospective places and look enthusiastic.
Ranches outside of town, buildings in town, run down,
spruced up… it didn't matter. He would just nod, cock his
head to one side, and write some notes down in a notebook
that he would never read again. Sometimes he said,
"Wow," if he was shown a view of some flat land that was
supposed to be beautiful. Other times he would
deliberately misinterpret some price by a factor of ten,
much to the delight of the prospective seller, and say,
"That seems reasonable." By then word had gotten around
Dansing—either that rich basketball guy and his pals were
visionaries, or they were suckers—but if the money was
good, nobody cared.

He even hopped in the sack with a more-than-willing wife of the guy who owned the lumberyard. The husband was out, and she was showing their house, which neighbored the lumberyard. Her husband was not around, she said again, standing close, but she was a partner in the business and was able to negotiate the value, and Reese could get a much better view of the property from the bedroom window. He grinned one of his grins, and that was it. Easy. By the time he made it back to the hotel where the party was, the whole town was waving at him when he walked by. He grinned.

Easy.

Chapter 24 - Stan

Hard to say about this town. No matter what he thought or what he thought might happen, it had a way of shifting that he really couldn't predict. He was driving The Shark through town, enjoying the sensation of driving again, window down, fresh air blowing in, listening to the rumble of the 440 V8. Stan was thinking about Loren, wondering what made some people good and some bad, but mostly thinking about whether he could afford it.

Money had a way of running low, and he would need gas money to get out of town, and enough for at least two weeks of thinking time to decide what else he should do with his life. He had just over one hundred seventy bucks. He should probably ration it out but thought about maybe eating a real meal at Gene's.

Gene's was the best restaurant in town. They specialized in three things: big steaks, enormous steaks, and impossibly large steaks that lapped over the plate's edges. All were served with a small wedge of lettuce, if you cared for that sort of thing, and a fork. Gene's motto was, *If you need a knife, it's too tough.* Patrons had no trouble discerning where they got their beef from because the cattle stood in blissful ignorance in a feedlot outside the back window. One saying goes, "If you want good seafood, eat by the ocean." The opposite is also true: the best steak in the world is not found in New York or San Francisco or London. It's found in a small place off the beaten path next to some cattle, in some flat spot in the middle of the country. Gene's was open, but so was the liquor store, so Stan drove there instead.

Chapter 25 - Dormeier

Dormeier had settled in to the task. The panic of the morning had faded, and he wondered what he had even been worried about. People see what they want to see, and it became obvious, painfully obvious, they wanted to see a multimillion-dollar casino. The crowd was gathering for free hors d'oeuvres at the bar. Dormeier's crisp stack of cash was being handed out freely, and locals stared at the newly minted hundreds greedily. News got around that free kegs were also set up, and people started showing up, crowding around, wanting to be close to the famous player and close to his free food.

Many had brought sheets of paper for him to sign. Word had gotten around about the size of his hands. Dormeier would lay his hand on a regular sheet of eight by eleven paper, and it would lap over all edges. Then he would trace around the hand and sign and date it. It was impressive.

The day was pretty nice. The damn wind had died down, and the sun was shining, so a little of the crowd had spilled out of the bar onto a patio by the street. As the sun set, what seemed like the whole town came to celebrate the start of something big. The crowning touch came when Reese elbowed him a little and pointed. Dormeier looked over and saw him.

The reporter guy from the radio station was coming out of a liquor store across the street with a bottle in a bag. Bobby whistled at him. When the reporter looked up, Reese laughed and raised an imaginary bottle to his mouth. The guy stopped. *What was his name… Stu?* Anyway, the way he just stood there… it was funny. He had heard the guy had gotten fired, so he was probably going to booze it up, drown his sorrows. Served the little weasel right. He laughed with Bobby.

What a loser.

Chapter 26 - Claire

Claire sighed into the aches and pains of a long day, home at last. She had found a small apartment across the alley from the café the day she started working there—close so she didn't need to use her beater of a car and saved on gas too. The place, in truth, wasn't much, but she didn't need that much, either. It did have one thing she liked, a tiny little balcony that opened off the kitchenette, big enough for a folding chair. On rare nice days, she propped the door open and would sit out there with an aluminum folding chair, maybe wrapped in a blanket, alone with her thoughts. She was sitting there now, feet propped up on the railing, wearing a pair of jeans and a sweatshirt, watching the day end, looking down the alley and thinking about Stan, and then, as if conjured by her thoughts, there he was, walking down the alley.

He stopped near a garbage can and threw away what looked like a bottle in a paper sack. She couldn't quite tell because the light was failing. Even at that distance from him, her hand automatically swept a wisp of hair away. He was saying something to himself, having an argument, it looked like, so he didn't see her until he was almost under her balcony. She was quiet watching him, and when he happened to glance up, they were maybe ten feet apart.

He stopped. He didn't stare, but he did look at her for quite some time. *Those eyes*. Finally he asked, "Would you have any interest in going for a walk?"

As natural as pouring him coffee, she smiled and said, "Let me get my coat."

Chapter 27 - Stan

He liked to watch her move. At the café, he would watch as best as he could without staring. She never seemed to hurry yet seemed to move in a way that reminded him of some sort of wild creature. She had strength and grace and economy of motion, as if she were performing a choreographed dance and not working a job. If she did look at him, it was always with a hint of humor, her eyes seeing something he couldn't. Her hair was a mess of brown curls tied back, with a tendril that always seemed to have escaped somehow. When she was next to him pouring coffee at the café, he was tempted to reach out and touch that hair, but he never had.

Just after smashing the bottle in anger, just after changing his mind again and deciding nothing was wrong with drinking one drink, just after deciding that he had enough money to buy another bottle, that he *needed* to buy

another bottle if he was going to get any sleep that night...
he looked up and saw her.

She was sitting on a small balcony—it must have
been her apartment. She was looking down at him with
that same gentle humorous look.

He looked up at her. He opened his mouth to say
something but then closed it. What could he say, that he
was a drunk and weak and a fool, that his life was a mess,
and there was no end in sight, and that as bad as this day
was he was still glad to see her? *She is beautiful.* Instead,
he asked if she wanted to go for a walk.

She brushed the brown curl behind her ear. "Let
me get my coat."

Chapter 28 - Claire

They wound up at the edge of town by the rails next to the abandoned AGI elevator. Four enormous gray-white towers reached up into the night sky. He stopped at one and looked at her. "Are you interested in seeing the stars?"

The night sky was on full display already, but she shrugged and nodded.

He rummaged near the base of the silo and found an aluminum ladder lying in the weeds.

"Still here from last fall," he said.

He kicked it loose from some ice encasing one end and propped it against the cement silo. He climbed up until he reached a padlocked grill covering the hatchway. The padlock was unlocked. After he swung the hatch open, she could see another set of rungs attached to the side of the silo, reaching up into the night air.

"Let's go."

She was not particularly afraid of heights, and she could see a protective cage around the rungs. Nevertheless, her heart was pounding a little as they climbed the concrete cliff—the physical exertion, the height, and his presence all had their effect. Every fifty feet or so, steel hatchways could be seen cut into the side of the silo. The fourth one was gaping open, and she had to be careful to step up and over it. The smell of musty, fermented grain drifted out of the hatchway.

His voice came up from below. "You ever hear that story about this elevator?"

She laughed. "Only about a thousand times. They said it was probably the most exciting thing that's happened around here in the past ten years."

"Is it true?"

She laughed again. "How should I know? It happened about four years ago, before I came. But that extension agent, whatshisname… Al, talks like it was yesterday. He must have told me that story three times, at least, even though I told him I've heard it before. He gets to the part where the ASCS agent finds out, and he starts laughing like it's the funniest thing he ever heard. One of the other waitresses that was there said he turned white as a sheet and quit that day, and the elevator lost their storage contract with the government the next month."

"Well, can you blame him? I'd quit too. That's a long way down. Is this the one?"

"Not sure about that. One of these four, I guess."

By then they had reached the top of the elevator, a thirty-foot pad of circular concrete with a small fence around the edge and several empty beer cans. Some brave soul had managed to wrangle a pipe-frame hammock up to the top. Surprisingly, the wind hadn't blown it off yet.

He pulled the hammock to the center of the circle.

His manners were formal and courteous. "Would you care to join me?"

Oh my. Men are trouble. Men are trouble.

Chapter29 - Stan

How curious this all is. Stan breathed the night air in deeply. The clean, light breeze mingled with the scent of her hair. They lay side by side on the hammock and looked up at the stars. Millions. Billions. He had never seen so many until he moved here, and far above the meager lights of Dansing, they were laid out as brilliant as the day God had sown them there, with a painful, breathtaking beauty that put a lump in his throat. The Milky Way glowed, a luminescent swath with all the constellations strewn about —some he knew, most he didn't. All circled slowly, accompanied by the sound of a prairie breeze.

How strange. This was one of the rare places where near silence could still exist. No whirring machines, no traffic, no planes, no music… two hundred feet above the empty plains, they seemed to be actually *inside* the heavens, looking down and across to the sea of stars.

The beauty of the night and the vastness of the sky made him feel impossibly small and alone. The busyness of his life and problems fell away one by one until there was just a dull yearning ache. *I am alone.* Parents gone, no siblings, a stranger in this town and soon to be a stranger somewhere else.

The memories of the past few hours and the knowledge of who he was swept over him. He began to weep, tears only at first, running down his cheeks, then silent sobs. He was mortified at his weakness in front of a stranger.

As if she had done it a hundred times before, she took his hand in hers and brushed her thumb over the back of it. The hammock rocked in the breeze, and her thumb matched its motion.

Eventually he whispered, "I have failed."

"Who?"

"Everyone." Then, taking a deep, shuddering breath, he told her everything about who he was, what dreams he had when he was younger, who he was supposed to be, and how he had betrayed it all. When he finished, the silence returned, the hammock rocked, and her thumb kept its gentle motion back and forth across the back of his hand.

Finally she spoke. "Stanley." That was the first time she had said his name, her voice soft and clear.

He could not look at her, partly ashamed to have been so weak, partly relieved to have shared some of his burden.

"Stanley Martin. We all got secrets. You have yours, and I have mine. You may have done many things, and maybe those things are true about who you are up to right now. But they are not about who you *will* be—at least they don't have to be." As she spoke, her words sounded like a speech she had made before, perhaps to herself. She looked up and away from him, her profile showing the edge of her own convictions.

She continued, "Even though I don't know if Stanley Martin is your real name, I know about people. And what I believe is that you are still a good man, still capable of great things."

In the clear night, their hearing became more acute, and the sounds far below started to drift up. A truck started. There was a faint sound of bar music, probably from the Holiday Inn. They rocked in the night, looking at the stars, listening to the small world below.

Finally, he said, "My name's not Martin, it's McGarvey. My real name is Stanley Martin McGarvey."

She whispered, "And my name's not Claire."

He turned to face her, gently tucked a wisp of hair behind her ear, and kissed her.
And with the moon their only witness, they shared their secrets far into the night.

Chapter 30 - Eddie

Eddie was working on The Dream that night. He had heard that some stations—heck, *most* stations—had skimmer machines, tape recorders hooked up to the mic, so when you flipped on the mic the machine started recording, and when you shut off the mic, it stopped. So you could listen to your own whole show in maybe ten minutes, all the spots and music cut out, ready to send down the road to other program directors in other markets looking for the next Rick Dees or Casey Kasem.

Sadly for Eddie, he did not have that equipment. What he did have was a fifteen-inch reel of 3M tape from the Chicago Symphony that played every Sunday. Eddie's job was to play it and then ship it back to Chicago in the box it had come in, tails out, within seven days. The instructions on the box said nothing about what he could do with the tape in that seven-day period. To Eddie, that meant he could erase the tape, record an hour of his show and cherry pick the best bits, then dub them down to a three- inch reel. Three-inch reels were tough to come by, but Stan Martin had found a great source from the Germany Tourism Board, or some outfit like that. *Germany Today* was a ten-minute show sent every week at fifteen inches per second on thick, high-quality 3M tape. No one listened to the show—because no one aired the show—but the tape was perfect. It even came with a questionnaire, which the jocks filled out with great humor.

"What do you think of *Germany Today?*"

"We love it!" "The highest quality!" "I wish it was longer." Humor at its finest.

After Eddie laboriously spliced up a killer three-minute tape, he would redub it over to another tape with no splices, so no one would know that he'd cherry picked it.

So far, after working night after night for almost fifteen months, Eddie had managed to send out exactly no tapes to other stations.

In truth, he was terrified of leaving. In truth, he liked dreaming and planning and plotting but never *doing*. He could never be a Stan Martin, a man he openly worshipped, talking to him whenever he came in, asking him about studio equipment, what the jocks were like in other markets, who was a good guy, who was a jerk, and most importantly, how much they got paid. Stan was not a gossip, not really much of a talker at all, to be truthful, but he saw the need in Eddie's questions, and he would answer a lot of them. The one question Eddie was afraid to ask was the one he wanted to ask every time he saw him. "Hey

Stan, do you think I'm any good?" He was afraid of the answer, so he'd never asked it.

Too bad about Stan. Even Eddie had heard. Because he slept late and worked late nights, he seldom heard any news, but Larry Karl stayed after, almost unheard of, hanging around late, just to make sure Eddie heard the details.

Larry was a jerk, and so was Happy Jack, and Eddie fantasized about punching both of them in the face. *Pow!* Ol' Larry wouldn't see it coming, then while he was doubled over, *wham!* would come the knee right into the face. Then he'd saunter into Happy Jack's office and dump the bleeding Larry on the desk and say he could take that job and shove it, then leave Happy Jack scrambling trying to fill the notorious Eddie Dangerous time slot.

Eddie smiled faintly at the image. He started dreaming again. How great it would be to get a call from Des Moines or even Sioux Falls. Some program director driving through on the interstate, scanning the dial, searching for talent. *Hell, maybe tonight would be the night!*

"K-D-A-N request line."

"Yeah, is this Eddie Dangerous?"

"You got him, man. What's your beef?"

"Hey, this is True Don Bleu. I'm driving across the interstate and picked up your show! Man, you are blowing my mind!"

He smiled even wider. *Why not?* His voice felt pretty good. He had heard some pretty good jokes. Of course, he could not actually take phone calls on the air — the board was not hooked up to the phone. But he had figured out how to patch the phones onto the reel-to-reel deck and record it there. So *if* he got a call, he could maybe record it while a song was playing, rewind it, and back-time it up the ramp of a song.

> *(music ramp starts)*
> *"Hey, Eddie!"*
> *"What's happenin', doll?"*
> *"I love your show!"*
> *"And I love that you love it!"*
> *"Hey, can you play Neutron Dance?"*
> *"The heat so hot, Eddie Dangerous blisters...*
> *Here you go, hon! The latest from the Pointer Sisters!"*
> *(vocals start)*

Nails the post! He burst out laughing at the dream and how real it all seemed. He looked over his shoulder at the big fat Chicago Symphony reel turning slowly on the deck, the red "record" light on.
This was going to be a big night.

Chapter 31 - Marie

Marie knew something was wrong. *One of the pills.* Almost immediately after she swallowed it down with the glass of bourbon, she knew. As she turned from the bar, she could feel things change. Her perception of her surroundings somehow detached from reality, slipped, like a gear with a broken tooth. The feeling was strange, as though she was watching a movie of herself. It did not cause fear or alarm, just a detached sort of curiosity, like she was hovering above her own self, and observing.

I wonder what she's going to do?

She seemed to be in a hotel somewhere. How come she couldn't remember that? She turned a full circle and stumbled a little. *What was this place anyway?* While the greater part of her mind puzzled over the mundane problem of identifying the hotel room, a smaller, more remote part of her brain seemed disturbed, worried about her life, wondering if the pill was trying to harm her in some way.

This fear for her life seemed almost laughable, considering she had been thinking about suicide off and on for years as a way to end the boredom. But she could see now in her detached, remote way, examining herself, that she did not want to die. *The pill, though—it's trying to kill me.* The small worried corner of her mind became alarmed, warning her, *begging* her to save herself.

The rest of her mind, drugged with alcohol and pills, struggled halfheartedly with the concept. *Am I really dying?*

She gazed across the room. About half a mile away, she saw the phone. The anxious part of her mind seemed obsessed with it, urging her to walk toward it. It was too far away, too much work.

What's the point?

Her mind broke away from the phone and cast about randomly—it seemed easier to just float that way.

Think! Why am I here? She frowned a little. It was something about John. And this town. She could remember the room and the press conference, seeing the way people reacted to the man they called The Big Door, either greedy for the fame or money he represented, or afraid of him. *It's always that way with John.*

But not that guy from the radio. Geez, that was funny, the way he almost ripped the whole thing down, whatever it was. John had come back from the conference, or whatever it was, shouting and cursing about some little guy from some two-bit radio station daring to ask questions. She knew enough about John to recognize when he was working an angle, a scheme, and the guy saw right through it—she could tell by the way it irritated John. Funny how she knew right away who he was talking about. She had scanned the crowd before heading up to the room and had seen him setting up his equipment. Their eyes locked as she walked by. He nodded and said formally, "Mrs. Dormeier." Odd that should make such an impression.

It was his eyes. His voice too. He was a smaller guy, run down even, but he was—more. Bigger than you thought at first.

She saw the phone again. She lurched to her feet, watching them curiously; they were so... slow. Slowly, casually, her feet walked across the carpet, then her hands seemed to come out of nowhere, floating in front of her, groping for... what?

A phone book. The panicking part of her mind seemed desperate about a phone book. The drawer under the phone had nothing, though. Just a Bible and a yellow magazine.

Yellow.

She stared at the magazine, trying to piece it together. That was funny too. This crummy little town— that little magazine *was* the phone book. *Funny.* She wanted to laugh, because it *was* funny, it really was, but the other part of her mind wouldn't let her. *Hurry.*

She looked at her hands—they felt like gloves. The yellow pages had maybe four pages, and only one BROADCASTERS entry. *Hmph.*

She tried to focus.

Maybe she should rest awhile.

Chapter 32 - Dormeier

Dormeier looked at the mess that was his hotel room, and he was furious. *Damn it*. He'd told Robinson to handle it. Told him he *had* to handle it while Dormeier was downstairs with Reese at the party. He should have had Reese do it—no, that would have been worse. Bobby was good to have in certain circumstances but not that one. Trying to gain some control of his emotions, Dormeier paced around the room.

Maybe he was worrying too much. He played the earlier events of the evening back in his mind. He was at the party, making sure he was seen by as many people as possible. Then Robinson came downstairs and told him in front of everybody that he was worried about his wife, that he hadn't heard anything after he knocked on the door.

Then Dormeier did his part. Looking concerned, he said maybe he'd better check. Then later, he ran downstairs demanding an ambulance, looking shocked after the paramedics, or whatever they called them around here, arrived and fussed over her cold body for a few minutes. "Dead," they said.

Then he was able to use his emotions to fly into a rage, to demand that everybody leave—to slam the door behind them and kick a piece of furniture.

Stupid bitch! He'd given her twice what should have worked. And mixed with the alcohol… But there she was, halfway across the floor, stuff strewn everywhere. She must have figured out something was wrong.

He kept breathing in and out, trying to put the lid back on his emotions, to hide the rage where it could not be seen, not until they were safely out of that dump.

Even at that hour of the night, some kind of cop or sheriff or something would probably be around, and he needed to think, to have a plan. He needed time alone with Robinson and Bobby to figure out what needed to happen next.

He kneeled next to her body and resisted the urge to kick it. What had she been able to do before she died?

He picked up the telephone receiver from next to her body and started to put it back on the cradle, when he stopped, curious. Holding the receiver to his ear, he listened. No dial tone. Frowning, he looked at the wall, wondering if the phone was still plugged in. It was. He held the receiver to his ear again. That time he could hear the faint sound of music.

Dammit! He softly hung up the phone and placed it back on the desk by the bed.

Whoever she had called had not hung up the phone, even after what had to have been at least a couple hours.

Who would do that? And what did they talk about?

He was worried and angry—a dangerous combination.

Chapter 33 - Reese

Reese hid a grin so Dormeier couldn't see it. He had never seen the Big Door so pissed, and he did not want to get on the wrong end of it. They were still inside the hotel room talking, so their voices were low, but Dormeier was leaning into Robinson's face, punching him in the chest with his finger, while he vented a stream of swear words.

You had to hand it to Robinson. He was taking it, face white, lips thin.

Bobby wondered what might happen if they both went at it. Robinson was younger, obviously in good shape, probably knew a bunch of Special Forces shit, but Dormeier... Dormeier was just *mean*. And he did not have a switch or filter, not when he was that mad.

He remembered back in the Hamptons when Dormeier had lit into a couple of spics that tried to help two drunken coeds that he and John were having fun with. That was back when Dormeier was still playing ball, so he was stronger then, but he picked one guy up and *broke* him over a fire hydrant then stomped on his face. The heel of his shoe hit the spic's nose with a loud crunching sound, like a wet board breaking. Then when the other guy tried to stop him, he just grabbed his head and *wrenched* it. That made a sound too, not one Bobby could describe but one he would never forget either. And it happened without a buildup or warning—it was just Dormeier going berserk.

Good thing they were just spics—no money, no background. Things blew over and got hushed up, the girls got bought off, and Bobby didn't say a thing because he wouldn't and because that was part of the fun of hanging around Dormeier.

Talking done, Dormeier paced around the room silently, at first quickly then slowing down as he capped his anger and formed a plan. A few minutes later, Dormeier told them what the plan was, and that time, Bobby could not suppress his grin.

It looked like he could have some fun too.

Saturday

Chapter 34 - Waltraub

Sheriff Stacey Waltraub slept well. He always did. Even though the phone call came late in the night. Not sure what he was supposed to do about it. The hotel said it was an accidental death. Probably was. But the guy was a multimillionaire and famous, so he ought to at least put in an appearance. He told the hotel he'd stop by in the morning, jotted a note on a pad of paper by his bedside so he wouldn't forget, and fell right back asleep.

He was not a worrier by nature, and life had proven out that worrying was a wasteful habit.

He awoke at five with no alarm, as always, swung his legs out of bed, glanced at the pad of paper, and started into his routine—the same routine he had developed early in life and gradually added on to: fifteen minutes stretching, three miles walking, some strength exercises from his performing days, one cup of coffee, one chapter out of the Bible, two scrambled eggs with toast, a five-minute cold shower, then put on the uniform he ironed last night, then out the door. Before he closed the door, he kissed Vangie's picture good-bye. "See you tonight, honey." Then he walked three blocks to the jailhouse, in by seven o'clock sharp.

Not one to hurry, he had a rolling gait based on a fussy hip and creaking cartilage. That plus a drooping mustache gave him the nickname Sheriff Walrus, a name he disliked but tolerated.

The office was worn but neat. One desk, some forms, a computer under a plastic cover—distrusted and unused—a wooden swivel chair that creaked and squeaked, and a cork board stuck full of things in orderly layers.

He left the fluorescent light off, pulled up the window shade, and looked out the window. He preferred natural light and would only resort to a small desk lamp if necessary.

He peered out the window, shook his head, and opened it a few inches. About half an hour before sunrise, he could make out what the thermometer attached to the window frame read—thirty-eight degrees. He shook his head again and grunted in semiamazement. *Not much of a wind, either.* He lifted a logbook out of the left-hand drawer and wrote the weather conditions in a crabbed hand underneath the date. Weather so calm and mild at that time of year made a person wonder. It could mean a real backlash of winter, a tornado, or an early spring—you just never knew. South Dakota plains weather was always puzzling and was a never-ending source of conversation if news was slow at the café, which it usually was. He thought about the phone call he had received the night before.

Won't be slow talk today.

He half smiled at the thought. First was the news of a rich ball player coming to town, then the press conference where the disk jockey at the radio station got himself fired, then talk of a land boom, making everybody, including himself, wonder if maybe they should try to sell a parcel of land or a building site.

And now the wife is dead, probably on a slab at Monty Cooper's place right now.

Well, he'd give the poor fella till about nine before stopping by and giving his condolences and maybe asking a few questions.

What those questions were, he did not know yet. He had been sheriff for twelve years but had never had a circumstance like this. Not built for speed in thought or movement, Stacey Waltraub did his best and only thinking slowly and methodically.

Pulling at his mustache, he leaned back in his chair and stared out the window.

*****

Stacey was nine years old when he switched families. His first family consisted of his mother and him. He had no memory of a father, nor were there any pictures or stories about him. Big for his age and mature beyond his years, Stacey provided for his mother as best he could. Because she drank a lot, this was hard to do. He spent many evenings looking for her at the bars she frequented or knocking on doors of men that were called old friends or uncles.

Some of the places he visited had people that took pity on him, offering him food or a place to stay. He never accepted a place to stay—the Studebaker was their home, and he didn't want his mother to come home and worry about where he was. Food, however, was different. Try as he might, he could not resist an offer for a meal. He was always ravenous, it seemed, and he knew food from his mother was a rare thing, not to be relied upon.

In other places, people weren't as nice. They ignored him or teased him, calling his mother names or trying to bait him into a fight, laughing at his angry face and surprisingly hard punches.

Small and elfin, Stacey's mother was as different from her son as chalk is from cheese. He was even tempered and calm, and she was as changeable as the weather. On the days she was sunny, she was a delight. She would call him her little big man, because already he was her size, and so mature for his age.

His happiest memory came right before the end, when she took him to a carnival. She had found money for two tickets to ride a rickety Ferris wheel and try a few of the games. Together, they had stood gaping as the strong man bent a horseshoe, and as the carnival barker ensured the crowd around them that inside the tent there were far greater wonders. Unusually observant for a boy of his age, Stacey could see the frayed and dingy costumes, the hard, worn look of the performers underneath the makeup, but he didn't care. He was enthralled, and that day stood out as the finest he had ever known.

And just like that, it changed. The very next day, she disappeared again. Worried, he looked all over town, in all the places she might be. He finally found her at a truck stop, drinking out of a bottle in a paper bag, sitting a booth, next to a big man with a flannel shirt and a cowboy hat.

"Hey, Mama…" He said it with concern and irritation, hours of pent-up worry vented in those two words.

"Shut up!" Just like that, she was out of the booth, pushing at him with both hands, snarling.

Confused, he backed away.

"Who's this kid?" the cowboy asked, still sitting down, upset at being interrupted.

"He's no one." His mother spoke quickly, turning back to the cowboy, trying to smooth things over.

"Mama..." Stacey tried again to approach his mother.

"Listen, you didn't tell me about no kid. I ain't got room for that." The cowboy looked unhappy and shook his head like a steer trying to back out of a fence.

"He ain't no one. Hang on," she said to the cowboy over her shoulder.

She turned back to Stacey and pulled him aside, her voice lowered into a fierce whisper. "You leave me alone, you hear? I am sick and tired of bein' held back by you and your whining. You shut up and leave me be."

She turned back to the cowboy, who was now standing, and pressed herself against him, "Let's go, Sugar—now." She pressed against the cowboy, and he smiled, the boy now forgotten.

Wounded, Stacey watched them leave money on the table and walk out to a semi parked outside. He walked outside the truck stop in time to see his mother in the passenger seat of the truck, her head just visible in the door window. She did not look at him or wave.

It was the last time he saw her.

Chapter 35 - Robinson

Not a good night. Dormeier had chewed his ass
half the night about the girl and the phone, worrying about
every possible thing. His own opinion was born from
many firefights in many places. *You make your plan, you
go over your plan, but once you're on the ground and in
the thick of it, the plan goes to hell in a hurry, and all you
can do is react.*

As far as the phone went... He'd given her a
double dose. He watched her drink it down with some Jim
Beam and Coke then went outside to stand watch. How
she was able to walk and dial a phone was beyond him,
and he fully doubted she was able to speak more than a
few syllables of gibberish.

Dormeier seemed in danger of making a classic
mistake, overreacting to perceived threats that did not
exist. Robinson took his punishment like a soldier but also
stood his ground for the mission, explaining that the risk
was still minimal, that overreacting was another mistake.

He was also reevaluating his own goals and
choices. He did not like how Dormeier was handling the
crisis, and was pondering a quick exit once they were back

home. He was also pondering smashing the grin off Reese's face. Geez, that guy rubbed him the wrong way. He was like a nervous hyena, always shrugging and grinning. And now he had a gun and was goofing around with it, never pointing it *at* Robinson but always pointing it *near* Robinson with a grin that said, "How do you like that?"

Yes. He had changed his mind. He was out. As soon as he was back home, he was gone. And if Reese happened to be there before he left, it might well be worth the risk to take care of Reese in a permanent way. With that thought, he suddenly grinned back at Reese.

Game on.

Chapter 36 - Reese

Reese could not believe how funny it was—almost too funny. They were sitting in the hotel room, nine in the morning, when there was a knock on the door and a guy from a movie walked in. Right out of central casting, Sheriff Podunk ambled in, cowboy hat in his hand, holster on his hip. He even had a tin star!

He even said, "Beg yore pardon."

Dormeier had been fretting all night long, but even he relaxed when that bozo walked in.
He was wide and thick front to back, not quite six feet, but two-sixty easy. He had a gut but not much of one. He was just a thick, slow cowboy, good for wrassling cattle and maybe pulling over speeders in Mayberry.

He had small watery eyes that were almost white, a sunburned face, and a big droopy mustache.

"I'm here to ask what happened, if you don't mind."

He pulled a small notebook out of a front pocket with a stub of a pencil.

For fifteen minutes, Dormeier told him, playing the part well, while the guy wrote things down slowly. He kept asking Dormeier to repeat some things over, writing them carefully like a first grader learning the alphabet.

Then he did the same with Robinson, then him.

Now Reese could have fun. "Shore, Sheriff," he said, taking on the man's slow mannerisms. Every once in a while, he would look concerned and slow down. "Are yuh gettin' it all down, Sheriff?"

Finally, he was done. He put the stub of a pencil and the pad back in his shirt pocket and looked at Dormeier.

"Thank you for your time, and my condolences on your loss. I lost my wife seven years ago, and it has been hard. Do you think you will be staying on?"

Dormeier looked troubled.

"Of course, we have had big plans for our casino project, but with Marie's death, we will obviously have to take some time to regroup and maybe come back another time. I'm not sure when, right now."

The sheriff nodded slowly.

"So it's possible you could come all the way out here on one day, have your wife die in the evening, and then leave and never come back." He turned and looked at Reese with his mournful eyes for a long, slow count of three.

Reese's grin was a little tighter. "What do you mean, Sheriff?"

That time Waltraub leaned a little closer to Reese, his expression wry, his drawl suddenly more pronounced:

"Jist gittin' it all down, son."

Chapter 37 - Waltraub

Smart-ass. He'd gotten used to it over time: smart-asses that got pulled over for speeding or smart-ass teenagers that got caught buying beer or throwing keggers. But it did wear on a man. Once on the circuit, he had been less tolerant of smart-asses. Somewhere—*Where was it, Indiana?*—some smart-ass with his girlfriend was making fun of Little Tony, asking if he had any money or if he was "short," making other comments about his height. Nothing was wrong with that—God knows they'd heard enough of it—it was the *way* he said it… maybe that plus the fact that it had been a long, hot day.

Anyway, Stacey had walked right over and hit him —once—breaking his jaw and cheekbone. Quickly, before the crowd could react, Stacey turned on his heel and walked two miles down the road and waited in a cornfield. Hofmeister was the boss of the carnival and had told them all that if there was ever any trouble, just walk out of town and wait to get picked up. Carneys had a way of getting in trouble, he said, and the best way to handle it was to break camp and leave town. No need to involve the police—they always sided with the locals anyway. So Stacey had waited in the cornfield, swatting flies and feeling miserable. The venting of his anger had made him feel worse, not better, and by the time the caravan of trucks had picked him up rolling out of town, he had learned a lesson. Talk was just talk and not worth the trouble, and from that day on he just let the words roll off him.

Still.

The way the smart-ass in the hotel suddenly sobered up when he asked about the death of that gal made him wonder about things. As he walked down the street, the sun was up and it looked to be a pleasant day.

Hmm.

His mind trailed back to the press conference. That radio fella, Martin, was stupid to get himself fired, stupid to look a gift horse in the mouth. *Lord knows the town needs any kind of help it can get.* He seemed to have jinxed the whole deal. With that gal dead, why would someone want to build a big casino on the same spot she died? It sure was a piece of bad luck. He stopped walking, leaned against the side of the old boarded-up JC Penney, and looked up at the sky.

Weird. Still no wind.

And warm. If the weather kept this up, it could hit seventy degrees. His right hand fidgeted, thumb rolling over the first and second fingers, a habit from his cigarette-rolling days. The nicotine urge was a long-ago thing, but when he needed to think, the habit of rolling a cig would come surging up.

Hmm. Must be the weather. Probably is.

But something wasn't right.

******

Carney workers got a rep. When he got older, Stacey would learn first-hand about that reputation, even have a hand in some of the edgier stuff. But that particular day, he did not know he was treading on thin ice and that beating up and scaring townies was great sport for many of the carney workers. All he knew was that he was hungry, and the smell of popcorn was more than he could resist. Even popcorn that was thrown away. Boxes of the stuff overflowed a garbage can on the other side of the fence next to Meester's Garage.

He was busy with his own hunger and sorrows and did not hear the man until it was too late.

"Hey, you little shit."

Stacey had heard menace before in people's voices, and he wheeled around to face the danger.

The man had a thin, pockmarked face and eyes like black spots. Stacey had seen him earlier running one of the rides and had avoided him as a dangerous man.

"C'mere, buddy." The man's voice grew oily as he maneuvered closer. Stacey glanced quickly around. The Fence was L shaped, and the garbage can was in the corner. The man had him trapped.

Keeping his eyes on him, Stacey reached for a half piece of brick that had been lying on the garbage can lid. The thin-faced man smiled, his eyes glinting dangerously.

"Stop." The deep voice came from behind the thin man, so Stacey could not see who had said it. Whoever it was had a thick accent—the word sounded more like "Schtopp."

"Hey, Otto!" The thin man immediately became small and servile. "Just havin' some fun with the townies."

Now the voice came into view, and Stacey could see that it belonged to the strong man, the one who was bending horseshoes at the carnival.

"Gett out." The two heavily accented words were layered with threats that made the thin-faced man swallow hard and scuttle away.

Still holding his half brick, Stacey looked up at the giant of a man, thick and meaty like a two-legged ox. His *head was shaved close, he had a large, drooping mustache, and his eyes were grey and clear as he looked down at Stacey.*

"Are you hunkry?"

Stacey said nothing.

Slowly, carefully, the giant man kneeled to the ground. He put his hands on his thighs and watched the boy with serene eyes.

"Vat iss wrong?"

Stacey's chin trembled. Angry, he sniffed and tried to rub the weakness out of his chin, but the more he tried, the more the emotions of the past few days came flooding over him. He sniffled, ashamed. Then he happened to look into the eyes of the strong man. Two lines of tears ran down the man's broad, open face.

"Vat iss wrong, my child?"

Overcome with sobs, Stacey dropped the brick and wilted into the dirt. With a shushing sound, the man named Otto picked him up and held him easily, patting him and rocking him while he cried, his body wracked with tears.

And that was where Stacey met his second family.

Chapter 38 - Stan

Amazing. He looked at the clock by the couch in the jock room. Almost noon! He had slept ten straight hours. Even though the couch was ratty and dilapidated, he felt refreshed and focused. He stared at the ceiling for a long moment, absorbing the sensation of... *what exactly?* He certainly was in bad straits right then—no money to speak of, no prospects, and no real chance of going anywhere. Yet he felt like something had clicked inside. Like a bad vertebrae had snapped into place somehow.

Yesterday, the best plan he'd had was driving away, if that could be called a plan. And, in truth, his plan was *still* to drive away—but the accidental meeting with Claire had changed him in a way he could not readily identify. She was like... medicine. No, like someone who'd reminded him of something important he'd forgotten. *Was it she who caused his different feeling, or was it what she said?* He smiled wryly to himself.

It figured that the day he got fired was the same day he found the first and only reason he had ever had to maybe stay. *Oh well, best forget about it.*

He had gas money and a good night of sleep, and he could probably make it to… *where?* He was thirty-eight years old. He had very little to speak of, just a few clothes, a few hundred bucks, and a car.

He washed his face in the sink, brushed his teeth, reapplied some deodorant, and sniffed his shirt. That would have to do. He was heading to the back door, when the door to the studio opened.

Eddie appeared.

"Hey, Stan! Got a minute? I want you to listen to something!"

Stan couldn't help but like Eddie, no matter how many questions he asked about places Stan had been, people Stan had known, and even how much money he made. To Stan, Eddie was like a big little boy with a mop of uncombed hair, all elbows and a dreamy look that always made it seem as though he had just gotten out of bed—which was almost always true. Eddie worked late nights and slept long and strange hours. He was new to town, so the lack of money and late nights meant that virtually no one knew who he was. Even people at the radio station rarely saw him, with the exception of Stan.

Stan would come in at the end of city council meetings, school board meetings, or county commission meetings, plug in his Marantz, and seek out whatever sound bite sounded a little less tedious than the others. Then he would write a fairly accurate and concise report of what potholes were being complained about, what book should be banned from the library, or what fence line was too close to the county road.

All of this was done under the watchful and worshipful eyes of Eddie Dangerous.

"Hey, Stan, whaddya think about KMOX?" he would ask.

That was merely a ruse. He would interchange all the clear-channel stations into the same question. What did

Stan think of 'CCO, 'KOA, 'WGN, or 'NAX, until Stan might slip a little, maybe mention a guy he knew, a place he worked, a style of manager, a format clock he liked. Then with a dreamy smile, Eddie would talk about what *he* would do if he worked that kind of gig, how he would jock a shift the *right* way, with good music, not that crap they played, and so on.

Another favorite thing was asking Stan to listen to his aircheck to help him craft a tape to send out.

That, Stan hated doing because of the one real gift Eddie had: Eddie could tell with unmerciful accuracy just how painful he sounded.

Most aircheck sessions ended quickly, with Eddie's smile fading, his eyes glistening with disappointment, and a "Well, thanks anyway, Stan."

Actually, Stan thought Eddie did have talent, but he made the same mistake many others had made over the years. He tried to imitate others instead of being himself. Even the ridiculous air name Eddie Dangerous should've been an easy thing to change, but Eddie's dreams of what he wanted to be died hard.

So it seemed kind of fitting that the last person Stan would see in Dansing was Eddie. And the last thing he would do was listen to an aircheck.

Eddie was in the prod studio, where commercials and other production were recorded. The prod studio should have been neat and organized, shelves of production music in neat rows, next to about twelve disks of sound effects—from door slams to car crashes. In this professional studio, a logbook should carefully note which music bed was used for which client, so there was no repeating bed music from spot to spot. The studio should have been a clean oasis where creative minds could shut a door and listen to a spot for the smallest flaw, and banks of new and shiny carts of various lengths sat erased and ready to record over. Those carts should have been next to a small, neat desk where a manual typewriter would be used to carefully note the length of each ad, the client, the cart number, and the last few words of the ad so the on-air jock could tell when the spot was ending. These cart labels should have been neatly stacked and ready by the typewriter, color coded for length — red labels for thirty-second commercials, blue for sixty, brown for fifteens.

What it was instead was a disaster. Piles of records were stacked in heaps, some in the jackets, some not. A few beat-up carts stood gap toothed in a mostly empty wall rack, and cart labels littered the floor. The logbook was flagrantly neglected, which resulted in heated arguments almost daily about which music bed belonged to which client. About every month Stan would attack the studio and restore order, a several-hour process that was roundly approved of by all staff members. Within a week it would fall back to chaos.

Oh well.

Eddie sat in the middle of the mess, oblivious. He was carefully cutting a piece of tape on a splicing board, other cut pieces of tape ribboning down the wall next to him, ready to be spliced together.

"This is it, Buddy!" Eddie's eyes were bright and happy. "I ain't sticking around here either! If you go, I go. Maybe not the same place, but not *this* place, not anymore! I got a killer check here, and after I splice this all together, I'm sending it on." He looked around in case anyone was listening and lowered his voice. "You know my friend Chris? In Mitchell? He got a copy of *R & R*, and there's a bunch of openings for night jocks in the classifieds."

A subscription to *R & R* was expensive and a quick way to lose jocks to other markets, so one of the smartest cost-saving moves that Happy Jack ever made was dropping it. This had caused outrage among the staff and talk, always talk, of the jocks pooling their money and getting their own subscription, but poverty and apathy had prevented that from ever happening.

Two tape decks were spinning slowly behind Eddie. One was a Chicago Symphony tape, and the other looked like a smaller tape, probably a *Germany Today* tape that Eddie was dubbing onto.

Stan pointed to the rack. "What are you dubbing?"

"Dang it!" Eddie reacted and shut off the smaller reel. "I was splicing out a song, and I bet I let it run too long." He dropped the monitor down into cue to check on the progress of the big tape. "Okay, I'll start it again after this drunk lady."

"Drunk lady?"

"Yeah, I thought it might make a great bit, but I'm probably gonna drop it. You can't hardly hear her, and what she says don't make sense."

The habit of looking for news, any news, anywhere and all of the time, is a hard one to break, and almost without thinking, Stan asked a question:

"Mind if I listen?"

Chapter 39 - Monty

Monty Cooper reached into his shirt pocket and felt the money for the hundredth time. He felt its reassuring crinkle and resisted the temptation to open it up and look at it again. Twelve grand. He slapped the steering wheel of the hearse and barked a laugh.

What the hell. He reached in and pulled it out. It was real, all right.

He slid it onto the dash by the cigarette lighter so he could admire it while driving. Twelve thousand freaking dollars!

I'm a genius! He thought about how his life had changed in the past day. Two days ago, he was looking at the funeral home insurance policy and thinking seriously about arson and skipping town. Today, driving down the road, he felt like a million bucks. *Or at least twelve grand.* He glanced in the rearview mirror at the casket and smiled all over again.

Back when he was a kid and his dad owned the firm, it was like this a lot. Full, lush funerals with fancy caskets and somber rows of mourners. His dad had a new Caddy every year and one of the nicest homes in town.

And like any good businessman, Monty Senior knew when to buy and sell and didn't let emotions get in the way. For example, when Monty's mom got too old, his dad traded her in for a newer model with fewer wrinkles and less baggage. And when he saw that Dansing was dying out, he renamed the firm Cooper and Son Mortuary, sent Monty off to get a mort science degree at the University of Minnesota, clapped him on the back when he returned from school, and took him down to the bank to sign the papers.

"All this is now yours, son!" He beamed with pride, gave Monty Junior a hug, and promptly relocated to Pilot Point, Texas, where he lived with his new wife and never returned phone messages.

Thanks, Dad. Monty was finding out the hard way about business and cash flow and all the other boring shit that had nothing to do with driving new cars and comforting grieving young widows. But things had taken a turn for the better when he met John Dormeier. Rich, grieving, rich, desperate, rich, trusting John Dormeier.

"I need your help. I don't care what it costs."

So, Monty had worked and reworked the estimate, figuring in costs for goods and services, factoring extra labor for weekend costs, "Emergency Personnel Costs"—eight hundred forty dollars. *Hah!* "Expedited County Records Retrieval Fee"—two hundred ten dollars.

He had worked most of the night, massaging his fees to extract as much from this case as was humanly possible, and the guy didn't even blink.

"I just want a quiet service with no paparazzi or nosy press intruding on my family's grief," he said.

"Yes. Absolutely." Monty had nodded sagely, like he was used to dealing with paparazzi and knew what a headache they were.

"I'm sure you would prefer to have secure payment." Dormeier then reached into the breast pocket of his blazer and took out a fat envelope.

I should have asked for fifteen thou. Monty shrugged at the memory. *What the heck—a guy's got to have standards.*

As it was, he stood to clear eleven grand pure profit. He grinned as he enunciated the fact to the casket in the back. "Eleven grand, Mrs. Dormeier! Thank you!"

If Monty knew a little bit about business, he would have in fairly short order figured that the vast majority of that eleven thousand of supposed profit needed to go to fixing his building, paying his loan, utilities, and taxes, and generally keeping his business afloat, but costs of business were boring. What was fun was dreaming of what he could do with eleven Gs.

The first thing might be to get rid of the sorry piece of crap he was driving. It was eighteen years old— too young to look like a classic antique, and far too old to be seen leading a funeral procession. His dad had bought it ten years back, from a funeral director in Huron who had bought it years before then from a funeral director in Sioux Falls, who had decided that a hearse older than four years was not up to their standard. True, it *looked* okay—no rust, only forty thousand miles—but the engine drank oil, and about every seal underneath was shot, making Monty's garage floor look like a skating rink.

That reminded him he should get a quart of 10w40 to drop in at the next gas station.

He thought about his route.

Plenty of time. The enormous clock on the dash was inexplicably accurate, ten minutes to noon, and the ribbon of highway stretched out to the horizon unimpeded. State law prohibited cremating a body for a full twenty-four hours, and she had probably died around midnight, twelve hours ago. Dormeier seemed concerned about the law, especially when he thought the crematory might not be open Sunday. Monty had frowned thoughtfully and decided that the dearly departed may even have died as early as ten o'clock, and said he thought he could arrange for a late-Saturday cremation... although it would certainly be more expensive.

Dormeier nodded, and Monty had then left to work his fiduciary magic.

Hah! Eleven grand!

His thoughts shifted back to the hearse. *No doubt about it, this clunker has to go.* True, no other funeral home probably wanted it, but maybe he could unload it in Rapid City or some other place where no one knew its provenance. *Maybe a painter or carpet layer, maybe a kid with a rock band. A couple thou, and so long, baby.*

He drummed the steering wheel, thinking. He was hungry, and the AC was shot. He couldn't believe the weather—it was almost *hot* outside. Damn Freon leaked out every winter and cost him a hundred bucks every spring to see him through the summer. *Oh well, not for long.* He'd let someone else deal with it. The sun was beating through the massive windshield, and although he had smelled worse, Marie Dormeier was doing what all corpses do, and it was getting a little close.

He calculated the miles. Four hours to Sturgis and the facility he planned on using. The retort sat behind the funeral home with a guy that would do it for two hundred bucks. Monty had not mentioned the massive mahogany casket that contained Marie Dormeier, figuring he would surprise him. Most cremations were handled in glorified refrigerator boxes, but Monty had this old, carved mahogany relic of a casket, shop worn, in storage, and with no more useful purpose except padding the bill. *Solid mahogany cremation casket—four thousand dollars.*

Anyway, there was no way he could start the cremation until ten in the evening, which meant he had six hours to kill, easy. He thought about a nice little place in Deadwood, which was pretty much on the way. It was known for its strong drinks and thick steaks and a little game going in back if you knew the guys. One of guys was a funeral director buddy that Monty would see at conventions, and the thought of showing off a little was tempting.

Six hours. Hell, plenty of time to have a few, cremate a body, and get back to comfort the grieving spouse.

What could go wrong?

Chapter 40 - Stan

The tape was a little muddy sounding, and the levels were wrong. Most boards had a phone line hooked up to a pot—check that, *every* other board that Stan had ever seen *anywhere* else had a way you could get a caller on the air with just a push of a button, but not there, not KDAN. To get a caller on the air, you needed to answer a phone, put it on hold, and then run a patch cord into the reel-to-reel and record it. Then you had to rewind it and play it back, and even then, you had to ride the levels, your voice being four times louder than the caller's.

But even with all that, the results of the phone call were tragically clear. Gears clicked and whirred inside Stanley's head as he listened:

A faint slurred voice: "Can you help me?"

Much louder, Eddie's voice: "Sure, whatcha want?"

Indecipherable words then "...killing me."

"You mean 'Killing Me Softly'?"

A slurred laugh and a sob. "Yeah. John is."

"Jonas? Jonas who? You mean Roberta Flack? She's the artist."

"No, my husband."

"So you want me to play this for your husband, Jonas?"

Soft sounds that could have been sniffling. "Can you help me?"

"Sure, lady, I'll see if I can find it. What's your name?"

A few seconds of silence… then Eddie stopped the tape.

"Bombed. Stinko. Never heard a drunk like that. Thought I might maybe use it as a bit, y'know, up the ramp of the song, but the levels are bad, and anyway, I couldn't find the record. It was in the wrong sleeve, and by the time I did find it, it was like the grooves were all messed up. You know Happy Jack's nephew, that fourteen-year-old kid, Sean? I seen him eating peanut-butter-and-jelly sandwiches, in the studio *on the air*." Eddie's sense of professional pride seemed to bristle at the memory. "It's like he uses the 45s as *plates*." Never upset for very long, Eddie's face changed, and he smiled his dreamy smile again. "Hey, that's good, platters like *platters*. Whaddaya think, Stan? Maybe I could use that as a bit."

Eddie prattled on while Stan stared at the tape.

"Hey, Eddie, can I have this tape for a minute?"

"Sure. I'm gonna take a break. I'm starving. You see the VFW dropped off some pancakes? They wanted a little publicity for the pancake feed this morning. There's plenty for both of us."

"No, that's okay. Can I have this studio?"

"Have at it." Eddie was already mostly out the door.

When Eddie left, Stan closed the door and rewound the reel. He listened to the tape again. That time he let the tape run, listening for the phone to disconnect. It didn't.

He let the big tape turn slowly, wondering how long it had taken Eddie to either disconnect the line or stop the tape. After a few more seconds, Stan fast-forwarded the tape, watching the meter. The big wheel of tape spun faster now. Easily twenty minutes of tape spun by with still no blip on the vu meter. Then with only about five minutes of tape on the reel, he saw a bounce on the vu meter.

He stopped the tape carefully, not wanting to stretch it, rewound it, and hit play.

He heard a faint background sound and turned up the volume on the monitor. It might have been a door, maybe some footsteps. Then a faint but clear voice that Stan immediately recognized from the previous morning.

"You stupid bitch. I should have killed you a long time ago."

Then after maybe a minute of shuffling, the receiver was picked up, and the faint sound of breathing emerged. Then Stan heard a click... and the dial tone.

Stan had been holding his breath without realizing it. He exhaled slowly, his mind whirling. Was that a murder he had just heard? He glanced nervously at the door behind him, stifling an urge to lock it. God in heaven, he could use a drink!

Chapter 41 - Stan

Now what? He stared at the strip of tape winding slowly around the reels. What it sounded like and what it probably was were miles apart, no doubt—probably some random drunk woman and a man who sounded like Dormeier.

Probably nothing, nothing at all.

But.

But what?

But if that was Dormeier's voice, then that could be Dormeier's wife. And if that was Dormeier's wife and she *was* dead, then that would probably put the whole casino thing at risk, and all that planning, the whole press conference, everything would have been for nothing. He would have driven out to the middle of nowhere for no...

And the coin dropped, and the hairs stood up on the back of his neck. With a rush of adrenaline, he suddenly knew why Dormeier was so angry at him at the press conference, why he had reacted with such venom, and why Stan had lost his job so quickly.

He reached over and stopped the tape, his hands shaking slightly. Again, he looked at the door behind him nervously.

He felt an immediate need for a drink—followed by an irrational desire to run and leave the tape, the station, the town, the girl… all of it behind.

The girl. Claire. She was a fool. She didn't know him as he knew himself. He was weak, a coward, a drunk, as his father had been before him.

As he was thinking, his hands were doing their own thing: erasing a small reel, loading it up on the other deck, dubbing it over, taking it off the reel, tails out, and putting it into a small tape box.

Twenty minutes it took, then he looked at the studio door for the fortieth time. With each passing minute, he became more and more certain that little piece of tape was very dangerous to have, worth killing for.

He shuddered.

Leave right now!

No. One dub is not safe enough. Make another.

He'll catch me and kill me.

He doesn't know the tape exists.

Where will I hide the two tapes?

Calm down! You have time.

The door flew open, and Stan jumped and wheeled at the same time.

Eddie was clutching his sides with mirth, eyes dancing, convulsed in silent laughter. "Man, did I get you! You should've seen the look on your face!"

Stan's terror turned to fury then washed away with complete relief.

"So, hey, whatcha workin' on that had you so focused?" Eddie got closer, curious.

"Nothing, just working on a story."

"What story? Why? Hey, you don't need to do nothing for this piece-of-crap station. Let 'em get their own stories."

Stan changed tack. "Yeah, I mean *stories*, for a demo tape. Hey, can you watch up front for me? I don't want Happy Jack or anyone to see me here, okay?"

"Sure thing," Eddie turned serious and left to watch the front door—for the exceedingly rare possibility that Happy Jack would show up on a Saturday afternoon.

Alone again, Stan looked at the tape in his hand, hefting its weight and pondering its importance. He wondered what should he do with it, where should he take it, and whether he should give it to someone or hide it in a safe spot.

He needed to know some things before he could decide.

Chapter 42 - Dormeier

All he had to do was wait. But waiting was what Dormeier hated most. He did the math for the umpteenth time in his head. Dead at ten. The undertaker picked up the body. The cremation should be done—he looked at his watch—in about nine hours. The sheriff could be a problem, but he couldn't do anything without a body. The phone was a nagging issue, but Robinson was probably right—she was too drunk to be taken seriously. She could never be understood. He needed to relax.

He looked at the clock in the hotel restaurant, a place that was trying to look like a galley in some kind of a pirate ship. Matey's was the name of the place, and the waitress had enough common sense to look ashamed of her blousy sleeves, leatherette shirt, and ridiculous pirate hat.

"You boys okay here?" She looked sympathetic. Word travels in a dumpy little town, and they might as well have had big neon name tags.

Robinson may have looked at her, but it was hard to say—he never took off those mirrored glasses, which was starting to really bug Dormeier.

Bobby grinned at the waitress. "Another beer, sunshine."

Oh well. Bobby grinned at anything in a skirt. Dormeier couldn't change much about that.
Relax. Relax.

"Say, Mr. Dormeier, I was really sorry to hear about your wife. She sounded like a real nice gal."

Robinson caught it first.

"*Sounded* nice? Did you meet Mrs. Dormeier?"

"No, not in person." The waitress blushed a little at the sudden attention of the three and explained herself.

"I'm not the normal waitress, but Sheila called in sick and asked if I could cover."

The three continued staring.

She went on, "Yeah, I usually work the desk overnights, like last night, so I'm pulling a double." She looked at the three.

No one seemed concerned about her workload.

"So anyway, I worked the switchboard, and then that's when she called the desk."

Dormeier's voice was soft and casual. "She called the front desk? Why?"

"She was looking for a number and couldn't find it, so I gave it to her."

Bobby's grin tightened a few notches.

"So who would she be looking to call in Dansing at that hour?"

"That's what I wondered." The waitress was happy to spill her knowledge. "Turns out she was looking for the radio station."

Robinson turned his mirrored gaze in her general direction. "Which radio station?"

That was cause for immediate mirth. "There's only one in town." She nodded her head down the street. "K-Dan."

Dormeier's brain was exploding with possibilities, all of them bad. His voice was concerned, like a widower wondering about his wife's final hours, but the knuckles were white on the hand that was gripping his beer bottle.

"Were you able to give her the phone number?"

"Oh, better than that!" The waitress was proud of her service to the customer. "I just patched her right through."

Chapter 43 - Reese

Reese was worried for a minute. After the broad in the stupid pirate uniform left the table, he saw Dormeier get that certain look in his eyes that he had seen more and more of over the years. The look said, "Let's think about this, and let's plan, and let's see what happens." Those looks were no fun and, more important, not what worked best. Bobby knew Dormeier better than Dormeier knew himself. Knew that he was most dangerous, *invincible*, when the old look took over, the angry, crazy look that meant what-the-hell and improvising.

Dormeier looked at him after the waitress had gone, gave him that crazy, angry glint, tossed him the keys to the rental car and said, "You got forty-five minutes."

Reese rolled his shoulders and smiled. *This is more like it*. Like in the old days, young and wild. No rules, just John and him, having fun, making it up as they went along.

Bobby grinned at the memory, a grin of pure wild joy.

This was going to be fun.

Chapter 44 - Eddie

When the buzzer sounded at the front, Eddie almost jumped out of his skin. *Dang it! Happy Jack!* No matter what he had told Stan, he did not really like confrontation and did not want to see Happy Jack—forget the bravado he'd claimed.

He thought about pretending he hadn't heard it, but curiosity won out.

Whew! It was not Happy Jack but some guy in a dark suit.

Eddie ambled down the shag carpet toward the front door and looked through the tattered film of the one-way glass. Visitors to the radio station pressed a button that buzzed in the back of the building and triggered a speaker system. The idea was you could find out someone's business on the intercom and buzz them in without leaving the studio. But Eddie usually walked to the door. He liked to talk to people and let them know that he was a DJ, a radio professional, in the flesh. A famous personality but humble and approachable at the same time.

Pretty big dude. Expensive suit. Even though he worked at a radio station, Eddie was pretty much in the dark about what was going on in and about Dansing. He knew virtually nobody in town and slept odd hours and—despite his plans—had even slept through the press conference the day before. *Looks like an out-of-towner.* He popped the door open a crack.

"Can I help you?"

The dude had slicked-back hair, the suit was expensive, and the shoes were the long, pointy Italian kind. He flashed open his wallet for a second and said, "Detective Reese, Federal Bureau of Fraud. I'm looking for some information. Can I come in?"

Fraud? What kind of fraud? Eddie looked at the dark glasses. They kind of looked like the kind secret service guys wore.

Intrigued and hopelessly innocent, Eddie opened the door. "Sure."

The dude shrugged his shoulders and grinned.

"Thanks."

Chapter 45 - Stan

The front of the sheriff's office was dark—no lights, no cars in front.

Figures. Stan had known it was a long shot when he left the radio station. He knew the county building would be closed, but he also knew that the sheriff kept odd, random hours. He had caught the sheriff a few times, very late at night, to ask a few questions.

Waltraub never appreciated that, of course, and he seldom gave him any more than some cursory one-syllable answers—and those never on the record. But that was okay—he just wanted to give him a tape and get the hell away.

But of course that's not going to happen today, is it?

He swore under his breath and went around the side of the brick addition. Waltraub's office was in the rear of the single-story addition to the courthouse. Sometimes he parked in back.

No car.

The door was locked.

He swore again.

He rummaged through the glove box of the Shark until he found a beat-up reporter's notebook.

The pencil with it had a broken tip. He swore. *Figures*. He looked in the glove box again. Nothing. Swearing again, he stood on his head, looking under the seat. Man, it was hot. Maybe down the road he'd get the AC boosted. The tips of his fingers felt something. He pulled it out—more irony—a neon-green KDAN pen. It had been Happy Jack's idea to buy a bunch of them for a promotion called Winning o' the Green on last St. Patty's Day. But they were all crap. The pens leaked, and the casing wouldn't stay screwed together long enough to write anything. He heard a door slam down the alley and looked up and around quickly. *Calm down. Nothing to worry about*.

He took the pen apart and scribbled with the cartridge until it was writing.

He left a blotchy note with the tape and stuffed it in the mail slot next to the door.

One down.

The second one was the long shot.

Mailing was the best option, but the post office was closed, for one thing, and for another, the postmaster hated his guts. He had done a story questioning why the postmaster's eighteen-year-old son was hired to deliver mail over some retired vets, and since then, the service he had gotten when he went to the post office window was suspect.

So he needed to find a place, some place out of the way, where the tape would be safe, would not raise suspicion and—most importantly, if worse came to worst and the tape was as dangerous as he thought it might be— would be so remote that no one would consider looking there.

And it had to be someone who liked him. In Dansing, that narrowed the possibilities down to exactly one.

Chapter 46 - Greta

"Wake up, darlin'." Jimmy's young and ageless voice was whispering in her ear.

Greta had been drowsing in the sun in an old metal lawn chair, the kind with tubular legs that you could rock in, next to her small back porch, watching the ever-changing colors of brown and blue and white and now even hints of green. She could sit and watch the changing light all day long, along with the change of seasons. Many times, she was startled to discover she had spent the whole day motionless, just watching the ever-changing prairie. *Another spring already? Maybe. Who could tell?*

"We better go, hon'." It was Jimmy. His voice was urgent this time, she could tell, not just to visit like other times.

She sniffed the air, pleased to have his company. "You think a storm's comin', Jimmy?"

I do.

"I'll be fine here." The house was plain but functional. Jimmy had found a bank of clay by a creek nearby, and together they had made the bricks mixed with dried prairie grass, heavy and solid, about twenty pounds apiece. A tornado had come by once, ripping up a corner of town, and torn the tin roof off, but the walls were as solid as Gibraltar. Even the harshest winter winds and temperatures did not dent the calm quiet of that house of theirs.

Not that kind of storm, darlin'. You better get ready. His voice had an edge, the kind of edge that meant danger and excitement, like when he took her hunting or hiking. At that sound, all the years fell away along with the ache in her bones, mostly.

"Will I be able to go with you this time?" Her voice ached with yearning.

Soon enough. In the meantime, somebody needs us.

Chapter 47 - Reese

"Is this about Happy... uh, John Warner?" The kid was all feet and elbows—he kind of reminded Reese of a lab pup he'd had as a kid.

"No. This is concerning an investigation we're running on a woman by the name of Margaret Wentworth." The lie came easily.

"She pretends to be in trouble. Calls certain numbers, asking for help, then cons them out of money, wire transfers, bank numbers, stuff like that. Anyway, we got a federal subpoena to pull her phone records and saw that she called a number for this building for about half an hour last night, and I'm looking for someone who might have taken the call."

"Last night?" The kid looked puzzled. "Well, I was working last night, and I don't think..." Then the kid broke into a smile of understanding. "Ohh... the *drunk* lady!"

Reese tried not to react.

"Tell me more."

"Yeah, this drunk lady called and was wanting me to play 'Killing me Softly' by Roberta Flack, y'know that one?"

Reese nodded.

"Well, that's what it sounded like she was asking for, but when Stan and I listened back to the tape, it sounded kinda weird, like maybe like you're saying, that she was trying to scam me into making me think she was in trouble or something."

Reese's grin tightened.

"Do you have this tape?"

"Sure!" The kid was eager to help the police.

The room he took him to was in the back and not visible from the front of the building, which was fine. The kid scooted a beat-up chair toward a battleship-gray relic with a reel of tape wound through it. He punched a button, and the reel started winding back, making high-pitched gibberish sounds. The kid punched another button, the reels slowed down, and then the kid punched a third button to stop the tape and a fourth to play it back.

Immediately Reese could hear Marie's voice. *Shit.*

"Is that her?" the kid asked.

"It appears that way. Could you get your friend Stan in here? I'd like to ask you both some questions."

"Nah." The kid frowned, his face clouding. "They canned him yesterday. He was covering some press conference, and he asked a question from that rich ball-player guy, you know the Big Door, John Dormeier? Anyway, Stan is a hell of a reporter—I don't care what people in this hick town say. He has been in Cincinnati, Chicago, you name it—"

Reese cut in. "And he heard this tape? What did he think?"

The kid got a cagey look. "Old Stan is good, but I'm not so dumb. I think he was real interested, like it was like you said—a scam or something. I came back in here while he was working, and he about jumped through his skin. He gets that kind of intense when he's working on a big story, and even though he said it was a demo tape for him landing another gig, I'm pretty sure he was making dubs of this tape."

"Did you say *dubs*?"

"Yeah, like dubbing over, duplicates, copies, you know? You copy 'em from this tape deck to this one then cut the tape and leave it on the tape backwards, or 'tails out.'" The kid was proud to show his knowledge. "That way, it keeps on the reel better and doesn't bleed sound so bad. At least that's what they said at Brown. That's the broadcast school I graduated from." He said the name of the school like it should mean something to Reese.

Reese dropped his voice. "Son, this is important. I need to talk to this Stan friend of yours and you while we still have time to catch this fraud ring. Do you know where he is and where the copies of the tape are?"

The kid nodded shrewdly. "Well, I'm pretty positive he took a copy to the sheriff's office, 'cause I saw him heading that way in the Shark—that's his car. And there's only one other place that he could take the other." He waited, hoping to build some drama.

Reese looked at him.

"There's this crazy old lady, Greta, who lives by the tower out of town. She calls and talks to all of us but Stan most—about ten times a day. Stan didn't say so, but if he wanted to keep some stuff for a story, I bet he'd keep it with her—she's looney." The kid wound his finger near the side of his head and gave Reese a significant look.

"How do you know he went there?"

He swung his hand out palm down and pointed through the wall. "The town's flat—on the other side of this wall you could see the radio tower about five miles out of town. She's got the land the tower's on—that's why she calls us all the time. Anyway, I saw a cloud of dust from the gravel road about fifteen minutes after he left. Who else would it be?"

"You seem pretty certain."

The kid flushed a little, like he had been caught. "Yeah, well, Stan writes things down a lot, a habit, you know? He's always writing little lists of stuff to do."

He gave Reese a small piece of paper with small neat writing. On it was written:

1: Stop by W Office.
2: Go see G
3: C?

"The W is for Waltraub. The G is for Greta—she's the crazy old lady by the tower. Not sure about what C is."

"And you think he made tapes for all these things?"

"Nah, just two. See?" He held up a reel with tape on it. "There's too much tape left on the reel for three dubs. He musta made just two."

Reese sized him up. "You're a clever young man... uh?"

"Eddie Chemelsky. My air name's Eddie Dangerous. You like it?"

Reese laughed. *This could work.* "Where do you think this friend of yours Stan'll go next?"

Eddie laughed with him. "That's easy... he'll come right back here." He grinned with his new friend. "Y'see, Stan's always forgetting stuff, especially when he's distracted or in a hurry... and look what he left this time!"

He held up a wallet, fat with cash. "He can't go anywhere without this!"

It's too easy.

Reese looked at his watch, only half an hour gone. The kid didn't suspect a thing, which wasn't as much fun as it could have been.

He shrugged his shoulders and smiled, having made a brilliant decision and fun too.

He pulled his .22 out of the back of his pants and hefted it. The kid's eyes grew wide.

"Hey, cool! You carry a piece, huh?"

"Yep"—Bobby grinned—"and a silencer too." He took a silencer out of his pants pocket. He'd gotten it a few years back 'cause screwing it on and shooting stuff was fun. He thought he might shoot at some prairie dogs or something, but having fun with this kid was even better. He screwed the silencer on slowly and grinned.

"You've been a big help, Eddie Dangerous."

The kid's eyes changed, and his mouth opened and closed twice as he finally got it. "Oh and hey, I remember he took a bunch more dubs too, and he called the dispatch at the sheriff, you know, and they're t-talkin about c-coming over any minute..."

His lies were strained and stammered.

"Hey, kid! You remind me of that Porky Pig!" Reese laughed in delight and shot Eddie Dangerous at close range with two hollow-point bullets. He would have to get rid of the cordite smell, but the bullets would expand inside Eddie, keeping all the blood inside. That would make it easier to clean up before Stan came back for his wallet. The kid's eyes were already starting to glaze over.

Reese laughed, leaned close to the dying boy, and raised his voice so the kid could hear the punch line-

"Ah- be-dee, bah-be-dee, bah-be-deee... Th-That's all folks!"

Chapter 48 - Robinson

Robinson was behind the radio station, carefully assessing the situation. *Whatever. What a cluster.* That Reese was a freaking psycho. Like you could pop a kid in a small town where everyone has eyes in the back of their head and just waltz away like nothing happened.

What a cluster.

Fortunately the back door was not going to be a problem. Whatever security it had was provided by a bungee cord that looped around the doorknob. The door was so badly sprung he doubted it could fit in the frame anymore. A look around the perimeter of the building looked promising as well—the possibility of potential witnesses was small. There were just a few battered and weather-beaten buildings within sight, and what looked like an abandoned feedlot, then the railroad tracks, and the wide-open prairie.

Oh well. It could still be done. Wait til dark, clear out the kid and the reporter, find a place to ditch the bodies. Better yet, dig out the bullets and light the place on fire. He went back in the building and rummaged around. Arson was easy if you worked only with materials present —no accelerants, or even a small-town fire marshal would figure it out. *Let's see. Put some Pop Tarts in that toaster over there. Rig it so it won't pop up, and in about four minutes you got a flame three feet tall and hot as hell.* The toaster already sat under a wooden shelf holding paper manuals and tape reels. *Perfect.* The place would be flames in five minutes.

Robinson shrugged. *What the hell.*

All he really needed was a few hours to get out of town and disappear. If he wanted, he could hire on with someone else, but after this fiasco, it might make more sense to take a leave of absence. Maybe a year or two, sitting on a beach somewhere thinking about his options. After making his plans Robinson returned to the back of the building where Dormeier was, all keyed up and jumpy. Robinson didn't like what he was seeing. He'd seen action with guys like that—like a freakin' bomb waiting to go off, likely to grab a gun and start spraying at enemies, friendlies, whoever was there. He looked at his watch, calculating how much longer he had to wait to start the fire and clean up. *Should be dark in a few hours.*

Reese was gone, thankfully. He'd been told to find the crazy old lady, get the tape, and come back. Dormeier had loomed over Reese and used his finger to punch into his chest the importance of not killing anyone, not creating any messes, and not making any kind of scene. And Reese'd had the good sense not to be a smart-ass and taken it.

But when Dormeier turned away and Reese glanced back, he flashed that shit-eating grin to Robinson as he sauntered out the back of the radio station.

What a cluster.

Chapter 49 - South Dakota

South Dakota ruins a lot of plans, thanks to its extreme weather. Oceans are the great buffer for temperature, and the coasts seldom stray out of their expected highs and lows. South Dakota, however, sits in the exact middle of the North American continent and holds a number of records, not necessarily for extremes, but for how fast things change.

Visitors passing through notice the amount of time locals spend talking about the weather. They smile indulgently at a folk simple minded enough to talk about barometric pressure and almanac predictions like they were life-and-death struggles. These same tourists might not be so smug if they actually knew how many of these people struggled with the weather in South Dakota and lost.

At the time Monty was gambling away his newfound riches, a weather system with the jaunty name of an Alberta Clipper entered the state, fresh out of the Arctic Circle. It hit the northwest corner towns of Buffalo and Lemmon at fifty miles an hour, with blasts of sideways snow and sleet and impossible wind-chill levels, picking

up steam as it went. Media outlets would call it The April
Fool's Day Blizzard, and it would even get some back-
page coverage on the coasts. Soon it would reach Monty
and Rapid City; then it would roar across two hours of
featureless prairie to Dansing, where it would definitely be
front-page news.

Chapter 50 - Monty

What a cluster. In the first place he hadn't meant to stay so long. But his buddy was there, and he couldn't resist showing him the mahogany in the back and then flashing him a stack of hundreds, wrapped in a little bundle just like in the movies. The steaks were good, and the little hottie working the drinks was so appreciative he tipped her a bill just to see the look on her face. "Here's a c-note," he said, all casual, as though he did it all the time. Her eyes grew wide, and he smiled. *That's how I do things.*

Then he headed to the game in back, where he was up a good thou, and the hottie showed her appreciation by keeping the drinks coming, plenty strong. Then... *What?* He was down by a couple, maybe three grand. Not too bad —he could still get it back. *Wait, what time is it?* A guy at the table was saying how cold it was, and another up by the bar was talking about a winter storm heading east at fifty miles an hour and how they were closing down the interstate by Rapid City already. Monty looked outside. *What?* Sure enough, the wind was back, howling out of the north. Across the street, a sign advertising the cost of fuel at the gas station was bent over double on its springs, its top banging on the gravel street. Monty could hear the clanging sound it made from inside the bar. Hard pellets of snow were hitting the window in front of Monty's face like pieces of sand. *What the hell?* It had been frickin' *hot* when he went in just a few short hours ago. He looked down at his stack of bills on the table, now loose in their wrapper. *This damn weather!*

Shit. A storm. And he was a good sixty miles away from the crematory. He'd better get going, and fast.

He lurched out of the bar toward the hearse. *Damn, what did that bitch put in those drinks?* He got in the car and closed the door. He could feel the wind rocking the hearse, and the white flecks of snow whipping by the window made it seem even colder than it was. *Damn.* He shivered involuntarily, started the car, and turned on the heater full blast, the defects of a poor air conditioner long forgotten. He stepped on the gas and swerved out of the lot, spitting gravel into the teeth of the wind.

Stupid weather.

Chapter 51 - Waltraub

One hundred twenty miles to the east of where Monty was, Stacey Waltraub came in the back entrance of the sheriff's office and saw the package on the floor. Hmm. He didn't remember having seen it before. He bent over and picked it up—no post mark, no address, just his name written in smudged ink across the front. He'd had an English teacher in the seventh grade with handwriting like that. For some vague reason, that made him a little less suspicious of the neat, square package.

He set it on his desk and looked at it. A cautious man by nature, Waltraub liked to think when he was faced with anything out of the ordinary. And although Dansing was light years away from letter bombs or conspiracy theories, the package with no postmark was unusual, and that meant it required careful thought.

He picked it up and felt it gently. It felt like a tape, the old reel type. Otto had a brother in Germany during the reconstruction that used to send tapes like that back and forth. As a boy, Waltraub could remember listening to the tapes and hearing news from West Germany from voices with thick accents trying to master English. He had memories of Otto recording *I Love Lucy* episodes to send back, with a big microphone next to the TV and strict whispered instructions from Otto to be as quiet as possible while the reels were turning.

Waltraub still had a few of the reels, some more than thirty years old. Every once in a while, when he was in the right mood, Waltraub would listen to them again, monologues from Otto's newly wed brother and his bride, talking about the Russians or the Berlin Airlift while their baby gurgled in the background. Now Otto and the brother were dead and the baby was grown, now with a baby of his own. *Funny how time flies.*

As sheriff, he had received plenty of anonymous messages of all kinds, usually from neighbors who got fed up with the illegal activities of other neighbors. Most of the illegal activities were barely misdemeanors, while others had merit. None had posed a direct threat to Waltraub. He shrugged and opened the package.

It was a tape, all right. A handwritten note in the same precise script was taped to it. "If John Dormeier's wife is dead, listen to this tape."

Hmm. Interesting. In a town like Dansing, everyone had already heard of the Dormeier woman's death. How would someone know enough to drop off a tape at his office on a Saturday and yet not know what everyone already knew?

Hmm.

Curiosity piqued, he walked to the janitor closet down the hall. On a shelf up high was a big cardboard box. He reached for it with a soft grunt and pulled it down.

Pretty dusty, it was his "halfway box." About every year, he filled it with stuff he hadn't used in years. There it would sit until he forgot what was in it. That made it easier to finish the trip and take it the rest of the way to the dump or to the Goodwill box by the senior center.

Inside was an old Wollensak reel-to-reel machine. He'd tried to give it to the grown-up baby in Germany so he could listen to the tapes but had never gotten a response, so it was in the halfway box, waiting for either a pardon or the landfill.

He lifted it out, pulled off the soft yellowed vinyl cover, and plugged it in. It was an old tube-type model that hummed as it warmed up. He whacked it a little on the side, and the hum died down some. He took up the tape, put it on the reel spindle, and threaded the tape around the playback heads and back onto a white plastic pick-up reel. Part of that was broken but not badly enough that it wouldn't work. Once it was threaded he punched the dark-gray play button.

Garble. He could not make heads or tails of it. *Tails*. Maybe it was on backwards. He remembered Otto saying a long time before that tape wound and shipped backwards kept better. He fast-forwarded the tape carefully so the broken take-up reel wouldn't catch on the tape. Once wound on the other reel, he switched the reels, rethreaded the tape, and hit the play button again. No good. Whatever it was sounded slow, as though the speed was all wrong. The Wollensak had two speeds, and neither made the tape understandable.

He rewound the tape, took it off the deck, and tapped it thoughtfully on the desktop. *Probably a waste of time*. Probably some smart-ass kid was having some fun with him.

He sighed and leaned back, the wooden swivel chair creaking.

It was Saturday. He had plenty of things to do not work related. No reason why he couldn't deal with it Monday. Maybe he could go down to the radio station then and have someone there help him; they probably had some tape machines with a higher speed.

He looked out the office window. The light had changed a little. *Must be clouds*. He looked at the note on the tape and reread it.

Dormeier.

Something about that fella wasn't right. The two guys with him weren't any better.

He looked outside again. The weather was definitely turning. The temp was no doubt dropping as well. He had already heard about winds and snow out farther west. Probably some fool was trying to get himself killed in a blizzard right now and would need some help. He looked at his jacket and wished it was thicker—he could wear the vest Vangie had given him as a Christmas present few years before she died, underneath the jacket, but it didn't fit right and was damn uncomfortable. He stepped outside to get a feel for the weather. The ragged flag on the pole tugged fitfully. Puffs of warm wind came from every direction, making Waltraub feel uneasy despite the heat. *Something is definitely not right.* No doubt the tape could wait. With the weather changing, he had a lot more pressing things to think about. He turned back to lock the door and stopped with his hand on the knob, wondering what was bothering him so much.

Chapter 52 - Reese

Life was good. The light of the sun shone down, hazy now, with clouds, but still a nice day. *Is this the place they call Big Sky Country? Somewhere out in one of these states.* Anyway, the play of clouds and sun too big to be seen by one pair of eyes made it easy to see why. By contrast the land seemed puny. The town ended in two blocks, and after that was a flat ribbon of road that headed to a horizon—no curves, no buildings, no nothing. The saying "It's not the edge of the world, but you could see it from here" came to his mind.

That particular part of the sidewalk was especially amusing. It was an honest-to-God boardwalk. He clomped along it as though he was in a western movie. He looked down at his Italian leather shoes. *Too bad.* He wished he had some cowboy boots. Maybe he would get some someday and maybe a hat, a black one like Clint Eastwood had. A .22 was the gun Reese preferred—less mess that way—but having a big old .45 with a satisfying boom and kick—he would have to look into that.

What the hell? He stopped and stared. Right in the middle of the block was an actual place with swinging doors like a saloon! True, behind those doors were regular glass doors. The saloon doors were glued on and the effect was cheesy, but the sight made him stop and grin.

The place was a café. He realized suddenly he was hungry. Starving. *Maybe a stack of pancakes or ham and eggs. Or maybe a tin plate of beans or a steak on a stick.* He laughed at the thought. At any rate he could eat now and get that tape and be back.

Plenty of time.

Chapter 53 - Stan

Greta Karns was waiting when he drove up, standing in the shade of the steel roof overhanging the adobe walls by a good two feet.

"Jimmy said you might be comin'." She was about five-foot-three and one hundred pounds, the size of a small boy. Weathered like a raisin in the sun, she could have been anywhere between fifty and ninety, but her quick, bird-like movements made Stan lean to the younger.

"Good afternoon, Mrs. Karns." Stan was a believer in formalities, and she was of the age that she appreciated it.

"He said he might come for me, my Jimmy. Said it might be soon."

Jimmy was her husband, dead and gone forty years easy, but she talked about him all the time. That, in the eyes of the town, made her crazy. But whatever Jimmy told her seemed to come true. She was never surprised—not by visitors, the weather... nothing—and that made her just a little bit creepy.

"This is important, huh?" She hefted the package Stan gave her, not asking what it was, not needing to ask, eyes clear and bright, staring into him as if he was a book she could read.

"It's not much. Just something to keep in a safe place." He gestured lamely, aware of how strange it must seem. She seemed unfazed.

"You've changed." She looked at him and nodded. "You are ready to be yourself again."

Stan unconsciously stepped back and looked away.

The woman carried on, ignoring his discomfort.

"You are a man. Good and bad mixed together, like all of them." She shot him a glance. "Jimmy likes you."

He shifted again, uncomfortable with the comment.

She paused and looked at him again. "I will not see you again, Stanley Martin. Go in peace."

She closed the door in his face and left him standing in the troubling heat.

"It's McGarvey. Stanley Martin McGarvey." He felt a need that she should know his real name.

The door said nothing back. But saying it felt better anyway.

He got back in the Shark and turned toward the gas station at the edge of town. He felt for his wallet.

Gone. He rolled his mind back and sighed as he remembered where he'd left it.

Too bad. He preferred to just leave without long drawn-out good-byes, and he did not look forward to saying good-bye to Eddie again.

Chapter 54 - Reese

Unbelievable. The hick town never ceased to amaze him. He sat at the counter by the wall, next to some redneck in coveralls and a cowboy hat—his face was exactly round, his hat was too small for his head, and his hand gripped his fork as if it was a handle and he was loading feed into his mouth. The place was full of rubes and school marms and suckers and fools.

He glanced at everyone in the mirror behind the counter. *Not a suit in sight*. He ordered three pancakes and some ham and eggs and was alarmed to see it come on a serving platter. The pancakes overlapped the platter edges and were shoving the eggs and ham off to the side. A glob of butter the size of a fist was melting into a fatty pool in the center of the pancakes. The whole thing must have topped out at eight thousand calories. Moonface was poking a similar amount of food into his face with leisurely efficiency, sweat pouring down his red face.

The only interesting thing was the waitress. She weaved her hips through the crowded diner, her movements smooth and lithe. She had the sinewy arms of an athlete and the careful eyes of someone who had worked long hours around men.

He peered over the counter she stood behind appreciatively and gave her one of his grins. "Hey, darling." He drawled the words like Gary Cooper. "How 'bout a little sugar for my coffee?"

She gave him a flat look and the sugar dispenser. *Sassy, huh?* That was okay—he liked a little sass. He gave her another grin, the one that said how much fun he liked to have with sassy women.

She involuntarily covered herself with a hand and suppressed a shudder. *Good.* Now he was ready to have a little fun.

She was coming down the counter, filling coffee mugs, and his was last. Just before she poured, he moved his cup, and coffee spilled on the counter.

"Oopsie. Better pour me some fresh."

Avoiding his eyes, she turned around to the Bunn and got another pot. With her back turned he stood and leaned over the counter to slap her sassy ass.

Crack!

She whirled around and whacked him on the side of the head with a glass coffee pot. Hot coffee scalded his face and splashed into his eyes.

"Bitch!" he shouted in rage, erupting from his stool.

Then he was stopped.

A huge hand was gripping his left forearm above the wrist, pinning it to the counter. He tried to wring it away but found he was being twisted into the countertop. Furious, he tried to strike out with his right hand but couldn't. The counter and his own body blocked the way.

The moonfaced cowboy in coveralls was calm and even had a measure of humor in his expression and voice. "You're not from around here, so you don't know." He leaned down a little closer to Reese as though he was talking to a stubborn child. Reese tried to butt his nose, but the man dodged his head back, easily avoiding the blow.

"Well, now." His voice had lost some of its humor. Casually, the hand—the color and size of a small ham— lifted up Reese's hand and slapped it down on the countertop, once, twice. *Crack crack!*

The heel of his left hand crunched as it hit the counter.

"Are you paying attention now, fella?"

The moon-faced man's grip tightened down in a way that made Reese turn white.

"This little gal is a favorite around here and a damn good waitress," the man explained gently. Behind him the café had grown silent. Many faces were curious, and none were sympathetic toward Reese.

"I think it's best you oughta pay for your meal and just go."

Reese grinned furiously then winced in pain as the moonfaced man gripped a little harder.

Reese clawed for the wallet in his back pocket wallet, plopped it on the counter, and painfully fished out a bill with one hand.

"That ten'll do. The rest could be your way of a tip and an apology; that sound fair?"

The cowboy, with the ease of loading a calf in a chute, switched the hand holding Reese with another equally massive one and, still pinning Rees against the counter with his bulk, reached around and grabbed the other hand, pinning both at his sides, with the cowboy behind.

An older cowboy chuckled at Reese. "Don't mess with him. He works with bulls down at the semen plant, and he's seen a lot rougher than you."

This infuriated Reese, who gave a savage backward kick back to the shins of the cowboy. Reese's heel made a hollow-knocking sound as it hit some sort of hard plastic shin guard.

The old cowboy clucked his tongue. "I bet *that* hurt. I tried to warn you, fella. Clem here probably gets kicked twenty times a day. He's got more armor than a tank."

The limping Reese was pushed toward the door, through a wave of interested faces, and then tossed into the street.

Infuriated, Reese caught himself, turned, and pointed his good finger first at the moonfaced man then at the girl, pantomiming a gun. "I'll be seeing you all."

The girl blanched, which made Reese feel better, but the moonfaced man merely smiled, which enraged Reese all over again.

Holding his throbbing hand, he limped toward his car and his gun. In the fifty feet from the café to the car door, he cooled down a bit, just enough to change the order of the people who would pay.

Yes, he would shoot the moonfaced man, and yes, he would visit the waitress and take his time, but first he needed to take care of a little business with that crazy old lady by the radio tower.

His plan at first had been to handle her quickly, her being old. But he changed his mind, thinking he might take his time. He needed to take more time to get control of himself, to have some fun, like with the kid at the radio, only longer and more... fun.

By the time he was headed out of town to the radio tower, his hand and foot were still throbbing, but Reese was grinning in anticipation.

Chapter 55 - Monty

He put the hearse in reverse and gunned it. He knew it was a hopeless exercise, but he was frustrated and angry. The snow was already piling up on the windshield, and he hadn't even been in the ditch more than two minutes.

The Northern Black Hills of South Dakota were famous for freaky snowstorms, and in his lifetime he had seen quite a few on the TV at night when the weatherman showed clips of the damage. He'd even been smack dab in the middle of it a few times before, and each time it was scary. And this one was scary too, really scary. He rolled down the window to try to see better. Snow pelted his face, blinding him to any signs of traffic, road signs... anything. He rolled up the window and tried to decide. The damn road had a crown to it and so many switchbacks, staying on it in such terrible conditions would be impossible. He should have taken a longer leg down to the interstate and over, but with the wind like that, that probably would have been shut down too. In truth he was lucky. He had been down that stretch enough to remember the drop offs — good thing he slipped over to the right side, because the other side was a good forty-foot drop down a steep grade. As it was, the ass of the hearse was hanging out onto the edge of the road with no visibility. A plow or truck could clip him easily, and then he would really be in trouble. Maybe if he goosed it, he could swerve into the ditch a little and try to find some level ground farther on and climb his way out again.

He alternated between low and reverse, trying to rock himself forward. The tired tranny lurched in and out of gears, the tires grabbing for traction. He gained some six inches at a time, and for a brief space of time, his efforts looked like they might work. With a surge, the hearse fishtailed sideways and spun five feet down the grade until it hit a three-foot snowball that was really a granite boulder with snow on it.

Steam erupted from the hood, invisible in the storm but audible nonetheless. *Shit. Just my luck.* Why couldn't he catch even a small break? He tried opening the door, but it jammed up against a clod of dirt or snow or something. *Double shit.* Well, at least he wasn't going to be hit from behind. With the stoic philosophy of the unlucky or stupid, Monty reassessed the situation.

It could have been worse. Yes, the casket was two feet behind him, safe and unburned. But he was only about fifty miles from Sturgis, and the storm could be over and melted in twelve hours. It could happen that fast. He was only a few miles from a gas station and a pickup — the hearse wasn't really needed at this point. After the storm died down, he could hoof it over to borrow or rent a pickup, load the casket in the back, and be down the road. Good thing he hadn't given Dormeier exact details on where the body was being taken. He could bluff it out later, saying he got stormed in after he got to the crematory.

True, it was windy, even in the relative shelter of the ditch. The hearse rocked with the blasts of the wind, and already he could see his breath as the warm air leaked out of the cab. The snow was a bitch too, piling around the hearse and leaking through cracks in the doors and windows. But at least it wasn't too cold—maybe around thirty degrees. He had some packing blankets in the back and could bundle up until the storm stopped. He kept a storm coat and a good pair of boots in the hearse for winter burials at wind-blown cemeteries, so the walking part wouldn't be that bad.

Better wait and see what happens. And heaven help the poor son of a bitch who was caught out with no shelter.

Chapter 56 - Dormeier

"So, you think he's just gonna walk right in?"

Dormeier asked the question in a way that both dismissed the possibility as ridiculous yet hoped that it actually would be that simple. Both he and Robinson were sitting in the dingy back room of the radio station next to a battleship-gray transmitter rack full of vintage equipment in various stages of disrepair. *What a dump.* The steel back door hung on a sprung frame, and a bungee cord hooked its way through an eye-bolt on the transmitter rack. *So much for security.* The light from outside could be seen in a crack all the way around the door, the gap as wide as an inch in some places. That bothered Dormeier in a way he couldn't explain, like he was the one that felt unsafe. He found himself fighting the urge to whisper.

Robinson sat on a padded stool next to what looked like a steel workbench, mirrored glasses on, face expressionless. Dormeier paced back and forth, in and out of another doorway that led into some sort of fraternity-style lounge area.

Dormeier hated, hated, *hated* waiting, and that kind of waiting was waiting of the worst sort. At least a breeze had picked up and the temperature had dropped. Dormeier was a big man who threw off a lot of heat. He disliked sweating, and anything above sixty-five degrees made him sweat. He had packed nothing but sweaters and a parka, expecting some kind of tundra, but the day was as flat as the land. The air had been stale and still, the sun a disk of hot brass, but now the breeze had blown in some clouds and with it some relief.

Robinson had been confident that that Martin guy would come back for his wallet, saying they should wait. And it had seemed like a good plan. Send Bobby out to cap the old lady at the radio tower, kill this reporter punk, and torch the station with the other kid in it. Robinson even thought there might be a storm blowing up, which would be even better.

But this waiting!

Dormeier looked at his watch for the fortieth time and started to repeat his question-

"So, you think…"

And then he did.

As if on cue, Martin opened the beat-up steel door and walked in, head down, in a hurry.

"Hey."

Dormeier said it with a sense of relief, like a worried parent for a truant child.

Martin was too far in the room to turn around. As his face changed expression, registering his mistake, Robinson quickly slid between him and the door.

A series of emotions flashed across Martin's face: surprise, shock, fear, then a careful blank look, the kind rabbits get when they sense danger.

Relief poured over Dormeier, and with the relief came the anger and joyous outrage that come with pent-up tension and emotion.

He stepped toward Martin and looked down at him. Time to catch up on things.

The smart thing would have been to kill him right away. Robison had a silenced .22 aimed right at him, ready to fire, but Dormeier was too angry, too wired, too *thrilled*, to end it right then.

"Hey, buddy." He punctuated his remark with a sharp backhand across the reporter's mouth.

Martin must have seen it coming because he moved his head with the blow then stepped in and, with a sharp jab, struck him in the Adam's apple with the web of his right hand.

Tears and pain and rage exploded from Dormeier, and he reached, grabbing Martin to catch his balance. Martin tried to stomp on his instep, but Dormeier hammered a fist down on his neck and stopped that nonsense. Then, in a feral rage, Dormeier picked him halfway off his feet and threw him across the room, where he struck the side of the workbench and fell.

"Stop it." Robinson said sharply. The command in his voice halted Dormeier.

Martin was curled up on the floor, gasping and in pain, and probably had a broken rib or two from hitting the bench.

"You can't beat him up too much—it might show after."

Dormeier's eyes were still smarting from the blow. He swallowed a few times to catch his breath. Robinson pressed his argument.

"The point is the objective. And the objective is to get out of this town the cleanest way possible."

He was right. The plan was over and complete, and he had won. No need to make things more difficult.

He walked over to the man gasping on the floor. *Definitely a few broken ribs*. He'd had a few in his playing days and knew how much they hurt.

Dormeier leaned over and pressed on the radio man's ribcage, and he gasped, his pain soothing Dormeier's nerves, calming him.

"C'mere, buddy." He heaved Martin to his feet and propped him against the wall, leaning over him and into him.

"You know something, asshole? Your nosy little questions have gotten you and your little friends killed. How's that feel?"

"Eddie'll call the sheriff." The words were gasped past a swollen lip.

"Who, that little punk at the door? Bobby plugged him an hour ago, after he told us about the tape copies."

Despair and pain flashed through Martin's eyes.

Dormeier enjoyed the look.

"Yeah, looks like game is over, radio man. Bobby's on the way to the radio tower, right now."

"The... sheriff has the other..."

"That fat old fool? I doubt if he's even literate. Where the hell is he gonna find a place to listen to a tape?"

Again, on cue, the answer to Dormeier's question was answered immediately.

The intercom squawked down the hall, and Sheriff Stacey Waltraub's unmistakable bass drawl sounded through the speaker.

"This is Sheriff Waltraub. Can someone there play a tape for me?"

Chapter 57 - Reese

He was grinning at the thought of what was to come, rubbing his throbbing hand, thinking about the look they get in their eyes when they *know* and how that made him feel.

The tower was easy to see but farther than he thought. *The distance plays trick out here.* The sky had turned gray now. Funny how much cooler things felt when there was no sun beating down.

He pulled right down a weedy gravel road—a field drive, really—brown spindles of weed stalks scraping the bottom of his car. It was like driving across a tabletop, so determining how visible his car might be to neighbors was hard. *Might need to pull it around back of the house later.* While he was thinking about where he might have to park, the decision was made for him by a small log across the drive, maybe eight inches in diameter. *Better not drive over it*—best to walk the last fifty yards or so, or maybe get out and drag it out of the way.

He stopped the car, put it in park, tried on one of his neighborly grins, and stepped out of the car. Leaving the door still open to shield his body, he stuck the .22 in the back waist of his pants. He could put on the silencer later. He didn't need it out there in the middle of nowhere —not a witness for miles—but he liked the effect it had. The look people got as he screwed it on, as they realized he was about to have some fun. The thought made him grin even wider as he closed the door. The wind was sharp, almost cold through his suit jacket.

A thin, reedy voice called out from a darkened doorway, "What you after, mister?"

"Howdy, ma'am," he called out to the house, wearing his best honest-man-looking-for-directions grin. He stepped forward with purpose across the sparse ground, more gravel than brown grass.

The sound of a shot surprised him, and the sharp crack of a bullet as it went by surprised him even more. He took a full two seconds to figure out that he'd been shot at.

What the hell?

"Stop right there, fella!"

His mouth was still open and slack. She'd *shot* at him!

"Now, lady, that's no way to..."

The second shot hit the gravel about three feet from his left foot and ricocheted off with a mean whine.

His indignation was replaced with anger.

"You can't just shoot somebody!" There was no irony in his voice.

"The hell I can't." He was close enough now to hear the bolt action. He dove to the right just in time, behind an old refrigerator lying on its side. The bullet hit the refrigerator high up, with a clanking sound, and Reese could see it had gone clean through about a foot over his head, a hole about the size of a quarter.

What the hell?

That old crazy lady was laughing.

"Jimmy warned me about you, fella!" the old lady sang out clear and high. "He taught me how to shoot this old Mauser. I learned to plug a can at two hundred yards, and I can surely plug you unless you get out of here."

Bobby was outraged. That was not the way it was supposed to go. *All right then, let's see what she does with a grill through the front door.*

As if she'd read his mind, a third bullet hit the radiator of his car. *Clank!* Then a fourth clipped his front bumper and went into a front tire. Its air hissed out, and the car listed to the side.

"Clear out, fella!" Her voice was clear and cheerful.

He was furious then. "I can wait out here all day, lady! You don't have a phone, a neighbor, or a prayer! I can wait as long as it takes!"

"I'd get a move on if I was you, fella! Storm's comin, and I ain't lettin' you in."

With that, heavy shutters banged closed. *Bitch!* The house was a low adobe type with heavy doors and heavy shutters, as though it had been built to withstand an Indian raid.

He cursed his weak .22 for what it could not do to those walls. Then he cursed again. She was right. A storm *was* coming: the sky, sunny a few hours before, was sullen and dark, the wind sharp and raw.

What the hell? Is that snow? Sure enough, small flecks of white were being driven by the wind. He half sobbed in frustration and anger. *Now that bitch is going to pay.* He looked off down the road to town.

Too far.

To the east, he saw what looked like a farmhouse —couldn't be more than half a mile or so if he cut across the field. He'd find some keys there, get a car, and come back. Still limping a little, Bobby Reese headed off across the field, grinning. *Get ready to suffer, Lady.*

Chapter 58 - Greta

"Is he gone, Jimmy?"

Yes, he is.

Greta sighed and lifted the Mauser from its tripod with an effort. She was tired. The excitement of preparing —the dragging of the log across the driveway, the setting up of the tripod—had carried her. Now with the danger over she was small and frail and so very tired.

"Can I go with you now, Jimmy?"

Hush, darlin'. Just rest for a while. This'll be a bad storm.

Chapter 59 - Reese

What the hell?

Reese could no longer see the farmhouse—or anything else, for that matter. What had seemed only half a mile was longer. The clods in the field were still warm but sticky with mud where the snow had melted. His fine Italian shoes had become sodden and caked with mud within in a few steps, and his thin socks were already soaked. The snow had been only a few flakes, but almost immediately, a wall of driving flakes had begun falling sideways, wet and cold, matting his hair, soaking his clothing.

And the wind!

It must have been fifty, maybe sixty miles an hour, pushing him off balance as he staggered against it.

He slipped and fell. The snow was everywhere, covering the uneven ground, making walking difficult. Scared now, Reese broke into a stumbling run, the horizon gone in a blanket of howling white. *Crack!* Reese fell, screaming in pain. His ankle had twisted, and tendons had popped. His right foot was bent at an odd angle, and any attempt at putting weight on it brought stabs of pain. Reese looked around, panicked. Wherever he looked was white.

One hour before, he'd been sweating and had the air conditioning on in his car. Now he was shivering uncontrollably, soaked to the skin, and about fifteen minutes away from being dead.

The weather.

All these hicks talked about was the weather. He'd thought it was because they were feeble minded or because life was so boring that there was nothing else to talk about, but now his numbed mind was beginning to grasp, too late, that they talked about the weather because it was the most dangerous thing they faced.

He started crawling. The knees of his fine worsted-wool slacks were torn through, and his hands and knees were scraped and bloody. Ten minutes later, he crawled into a barbed-wire fence that caught at his suit and cut his face. The blood from his cheek clotted with pellets of stinging snow. He stared at the fence, defeated.

He looked for the last time at the whiteness surrounding him.

What the hell?

Chapter 60 - Robinson

Robinson had planned for every possible option except for what happened.

When the squawk box announced the sheriff's arrival, everyone froze. A few seconds passed. Martin took a breath, maybe to shout, and Dormeier instinctively leaned into him. Any warning the reporter thought about shouting was stifled quickly by a gasp of pain.

Saying nothing, Robinson crossed the room and hit the buzzer underneath the squawk box, releasing the lock at the front door. Then he leveled the barrel of the .22 at the open door, controlled his breathing, and waited.

"Hello?" They could hear heavy boot steps somewhere in the front.

More clomping. *Where the hell is he?* Robinson looked at the light switch by the door, deciding which was better: to leave it on as a way to attract the sheriff or shut it off to give himself an advantage.

The clomping diminished; somewhere a door closed. Then nothing.

Robinson looked at Dormeier. Dormeier looked back.

Suddenly a cork board on the wall opened, so covered with papers and copy that neither had known it was yet another door—and Waltraub stepped through in midsentence "...anybody here? I tell you, it's bad outside..."

He stepped in just as Robinson wheeled around. Waltraub caught Robinson's face, recognized it, and was framing a question when Robinson fired twice at center of mass. At that exact second, a blast of wind blew against the back of the building, shaking the structure and whipping the steel door open, snapping the bungee cord.

Cold air and flurries of snow poured in, rattling papers, howling, and startling both Robinson and Dormeier. Robinson turned toward the sound.

Snow?

Then Waltraub fell to the floor, tipping over a large wastebasket. Robinson turned back toward Waltraub to refocus.

Before he could react or shoot, Dormeier shouted, "Hey!"

Hearing the warning in Dormeier's voice, he wheeled again back toward the door, raising his gun as he turned. For a split second, Robinson could see the scene framed perfectly by the back doorway: the steel door was blown open, the inexplicable snow was blowing through the door, and Martin was dashing for the opening. Then a gun flashed, too late and wide to the right, the bullet spattering harmlessly into the steel doorframe.

Then the moment was past. All he saw now was a white maelstrom of wind and snow, and the back of Martin disappearing into it.

Chapter 61 - Stan

Stan ran for his life. Time seemed to have slowed down, his legs pumping along as if he was running through molasses. He knew he was close to death, could feel it gaining on him, yet he had a detached feeling as well, as though he was watching a movie about himself. The wind was fierce and blowing snow into the left side of his face. He could not breathe, for his ribs sent stabbing pains into his side like a butcher knife, but stopping was definitely not an option. He heard the sound of gunshots and felt a snapping noise near his right ear, but mostly the overwhelming sensations were the wind and snow in his face, the stabbing pain in his rib cage, and fear.

The sound of the storm was deafening. Stan had covered news on the prairie through two winters. He knew how rare storms like that were, yet at the same time, how expected. That storm might not have happened in a hundred years, but freakish weather occurred all the time. About twice a year, a rare tornado, a rare flood, a rare hailstorm, a rare spring blizzard, a rare cold snap, all left the populace reeling. The infinite nastiness of nature, served up in an astonishing variety and dumped on Dansing at least twice a year.

The stabbing pain was extreme, and his legs felt like lead, yet he did not stop. He pressed on, knowing if he kept running into the storm, he would probably die alone on the prairie, but if he did stop he would most assuredly die of a bullet or a beating.

Pelting flakes, small and hard, stung his face and eyelashes. He could not see more than two feet, and what he could see were vague shadows and forms whipped by the wind.

He could not tell how far he had run or even in what direction. *Maybe I'm*—then he hit a building. He saw a shadow of it just before he hit, a glancing blow that knocked him sprawling into the snow. Dazed and in pain, face planted in about five inches of snow, he slid to a stop spread eagle, lungs rasping.

Just then, he saw a grayish form running by, feet falling in the drifting snow not more than four feet away. He got a glimpse only, maybe half a second. Whoever it was must have not looked his way and continued to run off into the storm.

The second sound came about five seconds later, that time to his right—a muffled thud and curse, about twenty feet away. Stan saw nothing but white snow, but the voice had definitely been Dormeier's.

Fear washed over him anew. He needed to move away but was afraid of being lost in the storm. Climbing to his feet in the snow, he approached the building painfully, hoping to work his way around it, maybe finding another building nearby. He reckoned he was probably by the bank or maybe the county building. One hand on the side of the building, he followed it around, looking for a doorway, moving away from where Dormeier was.

The building was familiar, and with a wash of fear, he realized what it was. He had been completely wrong— wrong direction, wrong distance, wrong everything. Instead of running parallel to the town's main street, he had been angling off and had hit the absolute last structure separating him from death on the prairie—the elevator.

Its large concrete face rose above him, disappearing into the snow. There would be nobody here to help him. The building was abandoned, and there were no doors, no way out of the storm. There was only...

He leaned against the snowy side of the building, hugging his hands to his side, shivering uncontrollably, trying to remember the layout of the structures. There were four cylindrical silos, each about two hundred feet tall. They all looked alike and all had the same ladder access he and Claire had used just a night before. He was freezing, probably dying, yet part of him marveled at how warm it had been just a few hours before.

Carefully, he circled the building, listening for Dormeier and looking up for a ladder. *There it is.* Its lowest rung was about three feet out of reach. It might as well have been a mile. He paused and looked out and away as far as he could in the face of the blizzard. If that was the same silo, there should be a ladder on the ground somewhere, maybe fifteen, twenty feet away. Guessing as best he could, he stepped forward, looking down to see how fast his footprints were filling. *Shit*. They were disappearing practically as soon as he made them. The snow was piled up, drifting as high as two feet or more in spots. He kicked around in the snow in a circle, trying to keep track of where the wind was coming from, trying to keep his bearings with the building now vanished in the driving snow. Kicking again, his foot caught the edge of something, and groping down, he found it was indeed the ladder.

Standing it up, he figured its length at ten feet. He dropped it in the likely direction of the elevator. He walked its length and reached out as far as he could. *This is ridiculous*. He saw white and only white, his own clothing matted white with snow. He was about to step off again, when he was saved by an unlikely source.

He heard a cough and a curse behind his left shoulder. *Shit!* Dormeier must have been doing the same thing he was, circling, looking for a door. He waited for a slow count of five, trying to control his shivering, then walked forward blindly in the direction of where he heard Dormeier's voice, into the side of the elevator again. He looked up and saw the elevator ladder to his right, set the aluminum ladder against the elevator, and started climbing until his bare hands reached the first snow-covered iron rung cast into the side of the elevator. When he was completely on the elevator ladder he reached down with his foot and tried to kick the other ladder away from the building, but his foot caught the top rung, and instead of falling directly away, it clattered against the elevator.

"Who's that?" Dormeier's voice, not more than ten feet away. He wanted to scream. It was over. No way down, trapped a few feet above the ground, he could only go up. Grimly, desperately, he started climbing, hoping that this was the right elevator and that the stories that Claire overheard at the café were true—or true enough.

Twenty feet up and still climbing, he heard a muffled curse then shout of triumph from below.

Chapter 62 - Dormeier

Shit, it's cold. This place is ridiculous. Two hours before, he'd been sweating, half-thinking about ditching his sport coat then deciding against it because he still had cash in the breast pocket. Now he was leaning up against some kind of concrete building with no windows or doors, snow up past his shins, feet numb in hundred-dollar silk socks and thousand-dollar Italian shoes. He grabbed his jacket around himself, wishing for the hundredth time he had brought his gun. He should have capped that little weasel as soon as he saw him. *Could have shot him easy.* He was within ten feet of him as they ran out the door, but then Dormeier had tripped and fallen. By the time he was up, Martin was gone, disappeared into the whiteness.

Now, who knew where he was, probably in some building right now warming up, spilling his guts. The thought made him so angry he could almost cry. Made him almost ignore the chills and wind and driving snow. What he would give to get his hands around that scrawny prick's neck and squeeze…

As an automatic response to the cold, he kept walking around the building, mainly to stay warm but partly to confirm what he was already sure of, that there was no door or window.

Then he heard a noise like a clattering of metal not more than ten feet away.

"Who's that?"

His feet were numb enough that when his foot hit something, it stung like a fastball off the neck of a bat. He looked down and saw a grid pattern in the snow. *What the hell?* It was a ladder. He did not remember that, and he was sure he had been around the building at least once. He wiped the clotted flakes of snow from his face and eyes and looked up and around. *There!* Metal ladder rungs climbing up the side of the building. Now he knew what this place was—it was one of those grain-storage silos that were parked all over the place out here. He had seen a few of them out by the edge of town. *That must be where I am.* Kneeling down, face close to the ground, Dormeier cupped his hand over his nearly frozen face, trying to get a better look. Footprints!

He yelled in triumph. *That little shit.* He grabbed the ladder out of the gale-driven snow and propped it under the elevator ladder.

Payback time, baby.

Chapter 63 - Stan

His hands were frozen claws, grabbing at the metal rungs. His feet were numb as well, and the rungs slippery enough that climbing was slower than he needed it to be. His ribs stabbed at him like an ice pick, but he kept on, driven by fear. Dormeier was down there and coming.

The shout of triumph from below had told him he was discovered, and now he could hear him climbing and shouting, "Run, you little shit, run!"

Stan needed something to throw but had nothing. The thought gave him pause, fear gave him courage, and adrenaline gave his trembling muscles strength they had not had. The shoes he wore were not quite right—he wished they'd been heavy boots—but they were steel toed, the kind mechanics wore, and heavy enough, he hoped.

Leaning with his back against the protective cage surrounding the ladder, he stopped, looked down through the blinding snow, and waited. About ten feet would be the right distance, but Stan didn't know how far he could see —far enough, he hoped.

Then suddenly he saw a face and hand.

Dormeier saw him at the same time and shouted in rage.

Aiming his feet, Stan let go and dropped. The distance was not ten feet, only five, not enough to knock the big man off. Worse, even though he connected with Dormeier's face, he slipped past his shoulders and stopped with his feet on the rungs at Dormeier's chest.

Berserk with pain and rage, blood streaming from his nose, Dormeier grabbed at Stan's retreating ankle. Savagely kicking, Stan connected with Dormeier's knuckles, the steel tip crushing a joint and freeing him for a split second. Fueled by a main-line shot of pure adrenaline, he hurled himself up the ladder two rungs at a time. Enraged, Dormeier caught at his shoe and ripped downward. Stan kicked the shoe off and ran up the ladder, one stocking foot leaving patterns of blood on the frozen rungs.

Climbing, climbing, Stan was heading for the last chance he had, a part of his mind wondering if he had the courage to gamble his life on a rumor.

****

Claire poured coffee for the afternoon crowd. Good old boys talking smart and telling stories. They tipped in nickels and dimes, but they reminded her of relatives she knew as a child, so she did not mind.

It was obvious that one of the farmers, a stocky, weather-beaten man named Henry, was telling a café favorite. Retold, polished, and retold again, but a story they all swore was true.

Henry was in the café years ago when it happened, and as a witness, he laid claim to the story and would not let others tell it if he was around.

"No... that's not how it was. It's wasn't in the afternoon, it was midmorning, 'cause I'd just heard the ten o'clock markets on the radio. I was coming in here to collect on a bet about two-dollar corn, when that inspector from the ASCS comes stormin' in, madder than hops, lookin' for Arnold."

"Who's Arnold?" Claire asked the question because she was curious and because she knew a good story needed a good audience.

"Arnold ran the elevator before it closed. Nice fella', kinda' lazy. He moved back to Cedar Rapids, still workin' in grain storage, but I doubt he'll ever be a manager again."

"Why? What happened?"

Henry looked impatient. "Which is why I'm tellin' the story, right?" Claire shrugged and waited for Henry to find his place again.

"So anyway, this guy comes in, swearing a blue streak and pointing to the elevator. 'You call yourself a manager? I swear you'll never get another government storage contract again!' So Arnold's all confused and trying to calm the fella down, but he's on a roll and will

not be coddled. 'I just been up to elevator four, checking out the grain, and you got it crusted over so bad, you can't even bust through it.'"

"I don't get it." Claire poured some coffee again, and Henry looked at her hard like she was kidding him. She shrugged, and Henry patiently explained.

"So when a fella sells his grain, a lot of times it's through a government contract, so he's really selling his grain to Uncle Sam. Since the government don't have enough bins to store it all, they contract with elevators to hold it for them."

Claire nodded.

"So anyway, when you put grain up, sometimes it's got too much moisture in it, depending on what kind of harvest it is, and to keep it from getting moldy, the elevator has to keep mixing it around, maybe drying it through a dryer. If he don't, then the grain rots, and the value goes down."

Claire nodded again. "That makes sense."

Henry continued, "And if you don't do a good job, a crust of moldy grain can form at the top of the grain, and if you don't bust it loose, you can lose a lot of grain."

"So is that what the inspector found?"

Henry nodded, smiling, because the story was about to reach its climax.

"That fella's face is red as a beet, telling Arnold, he'd been up there for over forty minutes trying to bust through the crust and see how bad the damage was, and he couldn't even break through."

This was Henry's favorite part. "So then Arnold gets all quiet and looks at the inspector and asks, 'Which *elevator were you in?' and the inspector, still shouting, says, 'Number four!' and points to the one he was in.*

"Then Arnold just shakes his head and says, 'That elevator was emptied four years ago. There ain't been grain in it since.'"

The table of farmers looked at Claire to see if she got it.

"You mean the only thing there was a crust of grain and nothing else?"

"Just a hundred and fifty feet of dust and cobwebs. That fella was trying his damnedest to kill himself on behalf of the US Government."

Claire felt the hairs rise up on the back of her neck.

"True story?"

"Swear to God."

"What happened to the inspector?"

"Turned white as a sheet and quit that very day."

"And what about the rotted grain?"

Henry shrugged. "The elevator closed pretty soon after that. Probably still there."

Chapter 64 - Waltraub

Waltraub rolled out from under the wastebasket and papers, stunned. He felt as though he'd been kicked in the chest. The room was cold, and papers were whirling around the room. A small drift of snow was collecting at the back door.

Grabbing for his gun, he fumbled it out of its holster. Not a gun man, he rarely wore one. He thought it rode too high on his waist for any kind of functional draw. In his long career, he had had only two incidences involving his gun—both had involved drunks grabbing for it while being questioned.

He marveled at why he'd even brought the gun in the first place. Something about events must have made a part of him spooked. Revolver drawn, he struggled painfully to his feet and listened carefully. As far as he could tell, he was alone. Wading through the papers and snow, Waltraub closed the steel door against the storm and possible danger. He could see that latching or locking it was impossible. He found a broken bungee cord and figured that was how people must have secured it. He tied the broken cord together and pulled the door closed.

Furious, the wind now shrieked and moaned around the cracks of the door. Other parts of the building groaned in harmony. There was no such thing as an airtight building in a storm like this.

Gun drawn, Waltraub now crept around the radio station, door to door, on cat feet, wondering where everybody was. He couldn't have been unconscious long —in fact, he didn't think he'd been out at all. He remembered his surprise at seeing the three of them together—Dormeier, Martin, and that fella with the sunglasses. Then he registered the menace on the face of Dormeier and that a gun was pointed at him, and just like that, he was down.

He fingered the front of his jacket and the holes in it. Six inches apart, chest high. His hand started shaking. Not more than half an hour before, he had been headed out to the radio station. He opened the door, saw the clouds, felt the change in the weather, and regretted he did not have a warmer coat for the storm that was sure to come.

The air had an unease to it, like the greenish light before a tornado but different. Waltraub had felt his hackles rise and looked at the unused vest on the coat rack. It was a gift from Vangie about ten years ago. A trouper had been shot up by Bell Fourche, and Vangie had found an outfit that sold bulletproof vests. She bought it for him, and he wore it exactly twice. It was hot and uncomfortable, and it chafed. He knocked some of the dust off and hefted it. *It'll add warmth anyway*. When he'd put it on, he'd felt a little silly but comforted nonetheless.

Twenty minutes later, here he was alive when he should have been dead. Thinking about it gave him the shivers. He was still pondering what part God or luck had in his fate, when he came across the body of the kid, whatshisname, lying in a pile of papers and crap in a recording room, the faint smell of cordite lingering. He'd been shot the same way, poor kid—no dusty bulletproof vest to save him, just shot for no reason he could tell.

The murder of an innocent boy made Waltraub angry and sad and powerless all at the same time. He found a phone and dialed some numbers, thinking the more folks he told, the more might be on the lookout, knowing that whatever the case, no real work would or could be done until the storm blew itself out, and heaven help whoever was caught in it.

Chapter 65 - Stan

The hatch was still open—not a crack as it had been the night before, but banging in the wind, smashing itself against the side of the elevator. He had no chance of missing it but also no chance of sneaking in and closing it behind him—the sprung hinges made sure of that.

Gasping for breath, Stan heaved himself through, the shooting pain in his side almost making him cry out. Perched on the lip of the hatch, legs dangling within, he was surprised at how warm the inside was. The freak storm had not yet had time to drive the stuffy air out of the cavernous void, and after the blinding whiteness of the storm, the blackness of the interior was complete.

Shit. He was one hundred fifty feet up anyway. *Maybe*. His feet felt around for some sort of foothold, some sort of ladder that went down inside, but he could find nothing. *Shit*. Dormeier was only seconds behind him.

Fighting down panic he tried to remember any details of the story. Was the cap of grain right below a hatch? Was it one hundred fifty feet underneath the cap or above the cap? If he was underneath the cap, he was dead. It was that simple—he would fall one hundred fifty feet through empty ink to splatter against a floor he couldn't even see coming. But if the cap was too far beneath him, he would fall too fast, hit the cap, and punch right through, the end result being the same. No doubt he never would have even made the attempt, but his time was up, and Dormeier made the decision for him.

Surging up from underneath, screaming in rage, Dormeier reached for him. Twisting to avoid his grasp, Stan lost his footing and fell.

Chapter 66 - Robinson

At first, he was simply reacting to the circumstances. He shot the sheriff and was going to finish the job with a double tap to the head, when the door flew open and the reporter ran. Then, quickly calculating odds —or maybe just reacting to something primal: run after what runs from you—Robinson was out the door about three seconds after Martin, one second after Dormeier. He fanned a few degrees to the left to catch him if he tried to feint, pistol out, looking for a shadow in the driving snow.

He started counting his paces, trying to control his adrenaline, forcing his will over his emotions. He kept checking and noting facts. Fact: temperature about thirty degrees and dropping. *Incredible.* A few hours ago it was around seventy. Fact: the wind was from the north, maybe northwest, and cut like a knife—already the side of his face was numb from the snow. His hand was stiff around the .22, which would affect his ability to fire. There were thick gobs of wet, heavy snow covering his eyes, his neck, in his shoes. At two hundred paces he stopped and listened. The howl of the wind was fierce and loud like a moaning beast—no way could he hear any sound of voices or footsteps. Fact: he was lost.

Breath rasping, he knelt for a spell, back hunched toward the wind. Quickly, he decided what his new objective was. It was not about killing Martin or following orders. It was surviving. He was in the middle of a whiteout with no shelter in sight, underdressed, clothing becoming soaked. The dropping temperature meant hypothermia was a very real and impending probability if he did not get lucky—and soon. He pocketed his .22 and stuffed his hands in his pants—the instructor at the tundra school had warned them about heat loss from the hands, neck, and head. Grimly taking a breath, he picked a direction, using the wind as a guide. Back to the wind, he stepped forward, counting his steps, one hundred at a time, checking his direction, fighting down his panic, hoping he would run into something.

Chapter 67 - Stan

The fall turned out to be about eight feet, enough to gain both momentum and panic. He hit the crust of grain in total darkness, not seeing it at all. His knees hit his chest, and his jaws clomped together, making him bite his tongue. Relief was immediate. *It was true!*

Quickly, though, the thought of his dangerous position took hold. Fighting panic, he scrabbled his way across the moldering grain, completely blind, seeking a wall and hopefully a handhold.

He hoped the crust was thicker at the edge—it made sense that it would be. The story was the ASCS agent was up there half an hour and more, probing and stomping through the rotten crust of grain, trying to get himself killed, before giving up. The only question was, *Would it still hold one person after all these years?*

The white square of light that was the hatch opening darkened with Dormeier's shadow. "Hello, asshole!" he shouted to the blackness below. "Are you dead yet?" Stanley stopped moving and tried to stop breathing, wishing his damn heart would stop *beating* in the name of God!

The shadow of Dormeier remained. Stan could see him close his eyes to adjust them to the darkness. *Good. There's a good chance he won't see me down here—the shadows are too thick.*

Click. Dormeier must have found a light switch.

The elevator was now bathed in an instant cold electric light, the blue of the mercury bulb buzzing against the wind outside.

"Well, looky here! A cock-a-roach!"

Dormeier's voice swelled with triumphant rage and bloodlust, his broken nose affecting his speech.

"You lost, asshole! Can you believe it? This freakin' blastass middle-of-nowhere freak show of a town, and you wind up giving me the most trouble!"

With the light on, a mound of grain about six feet high could be easily seen, tapering to the edge, about thirty feet across. Steel rungs could be seen next to the hatch where Dormeier was, going both up and down, the rest of the walls bare and rough.

"Stay up there!" Stan was torn between telling him the truth or hoping he would jump and maybe kill them both.

Dormeier's laugh rang out, high pitched and tinged with insanity. "Hey, asshole, I got a better idea. How 'bout a rassling match, you 'n' me, huh?"

Standing on the railing above the grain, Dormeier shouted like a wrestling announcer, stretching out each syllable, "Ladies and Gentlemen! It's time for the main event!" With that he leaped out onto the cone of grain, hitting it with a solid *whump*. Dust motes whirled around his ankles, and the pile of grain shuddered.

"In this corner, weighing two hundred and sixty pounds, John, The Big Door, Dormeier!" He sauntered over toward Stan, now on his hands and knees, desperately looking for a way to dodge. Dormeier timed his move, leaping onto Stanley with knees bent, landing on him with the full weight of his knees—crushing the air out of Stan, purposefully hitting the same damaged ribs.

Stanly cried out in pain, black spots swimming in front of his eyes.

"Hey there, little buddy. You okay?" Dormeier feigned concern as he knelt on Stanley's chest, grinding his knees back and forth. "You need to call for some help?" Dormeier's face clouded with mock worry. "Chee, buddy, I don't have a dime on me." He showed a thick envelope of bills, slapping them on Stan's face, like a bully stealing lunch money.

Pain washed over Stan, and he verged on unconsciousness. He felt like vomiting, then a small flame of anger swept up, pushing aside the pain and fear. *Why won't this creep just let me die?* Finding an opportunity and some final strength, he jabbed out and grabbed at Dormeier's crotch, finding his testicles and squeezing them in rage and desperation.

Yelling out in pain, Dormeier leaped to his feet and grabbed Stanley, jerking him up over his head and hurling him through the air.

Whump. Stanley landed in the middle of the pile and felt the mound shudder and quiver. Heart in his throat, he scrabbled across the floor of grain toward the open hatch.

"Oh no, you don't, asshole!" Dormeier saw him heading for the ladder rungs and ran across the pile of grain to finish the job.

Still scrambling, Stanley sensed Dormeier close behind, the fear of being caught fueling adrenaline to his body as he stretched, sprawling, for a steel ladder rung embedded in the silo wall. Just as he reached it, just as his fingers wrapped around it, the floor gave way.

There was a muffled crash and a blast of dust-choked air. The solid surface of rotted grain that had formed a crusted floor under Stan was now suddenly gone. With only his hands holding him up, he swung down hard, clutching the ladder rung for dear life. His broken ribs crashed against the rung below, and the pain almost made him lose his grip. Scrambling with his feet for a lower rung, Stan now stood at the top of an empty void that yawed beneath him.

The blue electric light from above now swirled through clouds of dust that made Stan cough with pain.

"What?"

The sound from behind Stan made him wheel around. The majority of the domed grain had fallen, but a thin, crusted lip remained ringing the silo, sticking to the rough concrete. On that ledge of rotten grain, Dormeier knelt , his large hands gripping at a lip of rough concrete left from when the elevator was casted.

The word had come as a question and a realization. Dormeier was wondering what had happened and was just now realizing how precarious his position was.

Seconds before, Stan's death was certain, inevitable. Now Dormeier was clinging for his life on a thin crusty shelf less than twelve feet from Stan and safety.

Stan's voice trembled with exhaustion and anger. "Hey, buddy—*now* come on over and get me."

With a surge of panic, Dormeier threw himself toward Stan, but he was too heavy, too late, and about one hundred fifty feet too high. With a shudder, the crust gave way.

With a shriek of terror, Dormeier pushed again off the wall with his feet toward the ladder but by the time momentum got him toward the steel rungs, he was twenty feet below Stan and accelerating. No hands, no matter how large and powerful, can hold a heavy man falling at that speed. He grabbed, hit, slipped, and continued to fall. John Dormeier, who did not know about the story from the café, or about the ASCS agent, or about the cap of moldering rotten grain, fell, twisting, twisting, down and down.

Chapter 68 - Robinson

He'd guessed wrong. He knew it. By then he should have reached town, but the direction he'd picked was wrong. He had slipped and twisted his knee, stepping in some kind of gopher or prairie-dog hole, and it throbbed a little but was mostly numb. He was numb all over then. He recognized the initial symptoms of hypothermia, the confusion and fatigue.

In other battles in other places, he had done some pretty miraculous things—carrying other wounded to safety, fighting when he could no longer fight. But he had no one else to fight for in the blizzard, just himself. And deep down inside him, Robinson decided he just wasn't worth it. He thought about the money he had saved, tried to focus on a thought that might see him through, but nothing seemed to work. His feet were like blocks of cement, heavy and lifeless.

A few minutes later, he stumbled into a fence. Falling, he got up clumsily and worked his way along it, thinking about the vague chance for a road, a building, and safety. But the fence came to one corner, and then quickly another... In the drive of snow and the haze of hypothermia, he could not figure out what that meant, so he sat down next to the fence to rest, just for a minute. He was shivering now, and his thoughts were abstract and vague. He watched the snow pile on top of his legs and tried to brush it away.

The snow was not that cold. Warm actually, like a blanket.

Thursday
Chapter 69 - Waltraub

A lot had happened in the past five days. The storm they were calling the Great April Fools Blizzard had hit at about four on Saturday afternoon and blew out by ten Sunday morning. The weather changed again, and the nine inches of wet snow was pretty much melted by Monday afternoon.

The discovery of the body of the kid at the radio station (Waltraub knew his name but couldn't pronounce it) had prompted a search, using the radio station as the center of the search hub. By five Monday afternoon, someone found a ladder tipped up by the abandoned grain elevator and a steel-toed shoe nearby.

Within fifteen minutes of that, a weak, cold, thirsty, and hungry Stanley McGarvey was found shivering next to a squashed pulp in John Dormeier's suit.

That let the hounds out. Within twenty-four hours, national news had descended on Dansing, picking the bones off the story. The bizarre April Fools Blizzard, the grisly April Fools Murders, the tape recording of Marie Dormeier's voice—every sordid detail was reported on every half hour. They showed helicopter shots of Reese sitting dead in a field, closer shots—gruesome, but ratings were ratings—showing him looking off with a dazed look on his dead face, and more puzzling shots of Robinson, who'd apparently circled the Catholic cemetery on the edge of town a few times before dying two hundred yards from safety. The best copy came from Monty Cooper, who replayed the conversations with Dormeier with lots of drama and innuendo. He was good for a few live shots— no more than that—standing next to where his hearse had gone into the ditch, a hundred miles west of Dansing. Last he'd heard, Monty was trying to sell the mahogany casket that held Dormeier's murdered wife to a roadside museum out of Texas.

Of course they tried to pick some juicy bits off of Waltraub but found the picking sadly boring. He spoke slowly and was prone to single syllables, and when asked why he wore a bulletproof vest, he merely shrugged.

McGarvey was worse. He spoke to no television media. Even when cleared by the doctor to do so, he talked only to radio reporters. There were two, a guy flown out from CBS radio, a passing acquaintance Stan knew from long ago and a long-time radio reporter out of Sioux Falls named Chris Holmberg, who called in for a phone bit, and Hal From-the-Gazette. All national media was forced to quote these small local sources, something that Waltraub imagined greatly pleased McGarvey. It kind of pleased him as well. McGarvey had turned out to be someone that Waltraub hadn't figured on, a man who tended to be overlooked or underestimated.

Oh well. The time to reassess the qualities of Stan McGarvey was past. He was checking out of the hospital that day and should be on the road to somewhere else by that night. None of his business, of course, yet he felt compelled to have a final reckoning, so hat in hand, he walked down the hall of the small county hospital to say what was on his mind.

Chapter 70 - Stan

Breathing still hurt like hell. He had had a little fight with some nurses who wanted to bind him up like a turkey. His own opinion was that breathing was something he needed to do, no matter how painful—along with walking, thank you very much. The doctor came in and settled it, saying the binding was mainly for the pain, so if Stan wanted to walk around in pain, sit in pain, and be in pain, that was his business.

He *did* want to be in pain. He deserved it. He'd liked Eddie and perhaps been the only person in Dansing who'd had more than a fleeting conversation with him. Of all the people who wanted to see Stan, the only one he spent any real time with was Eddie's mother, heartbroken and inconsolable, who drove up from Decatur all through the night and was arranging to have Eddie sent home. She cried a lot as Stan explained what he thought happened and apologized for his role in Eddie's death. His words and sorrow didn't seem to help much, and she left more grief stricken than she'd been when she arrived.

The other was Claire. She was there when he woke up in the hospital. Together they did more sitting than talking—she held his hand and occasionally fixed a pillow or fetched a glass of water. She seemed to sense that Stan preferred being left alone when recovering, and that suited her well since she was not the fussing type. Finally, they came to an agreement, then there was more silence, this time the more companionable type. Then she stood up, squeezed his hand, and said, "I will see you." She kissed his forehead and walked out and was gone. That caused a different kind of pain, a kind that he was not used to and had a harder time dealing with.

On the fifth day, they let him shower and shave and put on street clothes. He was ready to disappear, the thought of a cool beer or grapefruit and vodka sitting in the back of his mind, waiting—a fight he was still not sure he was strong enough for.

He was sitting by his bed, waiting for the nurse, when the sheriff appeared at his door.

"Can I come in?"

Of course, Stan had heard by then that Waltraub was not dead, that he'd been wearing a bulletproof vest. The reporter in him wanted to ask some questions since it was known about town that Waltraub never wore a vest or a gun, but he was tired of being curious and decided that he didn't care.

"Sure."

Stanley motioned him to come in. The room was small and sterile, with no other chair, so the sheriff instead eased up against the doorjamb.

"I figured you would be heading out of town, and there was a matter of a few things that should be settled up before you do."

Stan gazed at him, waiting for him to continue.

The sheriff shifted his weight and cleared his throat a little uncomfortably. "We've checked with all concerned—there'll be no charges for you to worry about. A little bit on trespassing from the bank that now owns the elevator, but we smoothed that over."

Stan's gaze remained unflinching, and the sheriff hurried on.

"Not that it affects you necessarily, but that fella that froze to death out by Greta's house… Turns out he was armed and most likely the one who killed that young boy at the radio station. Anything she did can be put down to protecting property and self-defense."

The sheriff continued, "But there is a question of outstanding debts."

Stan raised his eyebrows slightly.

"You were technically not an employee of the radio station, and therefore their insurance company has rejected any claim you might have here, and the bill is, uh"—he consulted a piece of paper—"somewhere around fifteen hundred dollars."

Before Stan could react, the sheriff raised a hand and got to why he'd come in the first place.

"I heard you cleaned out your checking account, and others tell me you were known to be a fella who preferred to pay cash."

He tossed a thick manila envelope on the bed. "We found this all over the floor of the elevator. We cleaned up what we needed to and put it all in there, just over eleven thousand, mostly in hundreds. I figured it was either yours or that murdering son of a bitch, and since he's dead, and I have no desire to ask his estate, I'm gonna assume it's yours. And being that the tight-ass company you worked for doesn't have the common decency to help a fella that came *this* close to getting killed, I figured I'd pay the hospital bills out of that so you never have to see this sorry town again. The rest of it's right there."
He paused. He was not used to speaking that long or letting his emotions get the best of him.

Stan was surprised—more so when the sheriff walked over to his bed, holding out a thick, calloused hand.

"I wouldn't mind shaking your hand."

Confused, Stanley put out his hand, much smaller in the sheriff's.

The sheriff looked him in the eye. "To my mind, you're some kind of hero." Then, nodding his head, he put on his hat and walked out the door.

Epilogue

The town was named Lake City, a small town but a different kind of small. Near Madison, Wisconsin, these people slept here at night and drove to the better-paying jobs, bringing prosperity home. The streets were well paved, the homes kept up and sometimes opulent. The evening sky still had stars, but humidity and light pollution made them faint in comparison.

A side street was tree lined, and the Shark sat idling in the shadows. It was finely tuned and polished now. The mechanic who did the work solidified the relationship when he patted the hood and said to Stan, "Nice car."

The sun had set about an hour earlier and a streetlight illuminated the church parking lot. A sign on the church door read, "AA meeting tonight."

Stan sat in the car, lights out, listening to it idle, lost in thought. His new job was better than the last—an old connection had come through. The station tour earlier *that day had brought back memories of better days and a glimmer of a better future.*

For at least ten minutes, he sat in the dark, thinking—thinking of people, thinking about fears, thinking that the taste of vodka could make everything better and everything worse.

Mostly, he thought about the stars that blew across the prairie, carried on a clean, crisp wind.

He sighed, shut off the motor, and walked into the church.

An excerpt from the second novel in the Dead Air series -
Dead Heat*- now available on Kindle Direct*

Claire

Good Lord, she was tired. It had not been unusually busy
at the café. She'd been on her feet since five-thirty that
morning, but that was just a typical day, and the hard, hot
work was of no consequence normally.

Must be coming down with something.

Yet the woman known as Claire would not shirk any work,
no matter how tough the job or how sick she felt. She
owed that to her father, at least she knew how to work.

"Claire, collect the tab off Harold and the boys and get
them outta here." Doris was the owner of the café, a stout,
florid woman with the forearms and voice of a professional
wrestler. "I wanna close before the next ice age."

Doris was a stickler for many things, and closing on time
was one of them. The café served breakfast and lunch only,
defined as five thirty in the morning to two in the afternoon
Monday through Saturday, and hungry diners who wanted
to be fed outside of those times were shown a yellowed
sign by a frowning Doris, the sign stated, "Hungry? Our
after-hours cook is Helen Waite. If you want to eat, go to
Helen Waite."

Claire tucked a tendril of curly dark hair behind an ear and headed over to the last occupied table, which held a foursome of retired ranchers playing dice.

"It's two o'clock, boys. Let's close up so we can see you again tomorrow."

Harold had the mouth. "C'mon, Claire. Lemme take you home."

"I got my own home, Harold, and I'd like to get there."

Sixty and plump, Harold was probably the most harmless man Claire dealt with, but he still liked to flirt.

"Where have you been all my life?"
She gave a deadpan answer. "Well, for the first half, I wasn't born yet." That got a groan of approval from the table—Claire was the café's main source of entertainment and a favorite reason to linger.

Harold was not done yet. "Oh, Claire. Tell me the three words I need to hear."

Claire placed both hands on the table and leaned over. "Leave. A. Tip."

All four burst out laughing, and she joined in. A tip from them would probably be no greater than small change, but that was okay—she'd grown up around ranchers like them and knew their ways.

Once they were out, Claire threw the lock on the front door and pulled down the Venetian blinds.

Now came the cleanup. Doris, Claire, and Beatrice—a spare-framed woman with a smoker's cough—moved about with the brisk, efficient movements of people who knew exactly what to do and with the economy of words of people who wanted it done quickly.

Claire did a quick sweep of the floor, gathering menus and discarded napkins as she went. Doris shut down the oven and got the two big cast-iron sinks filled, the first with hot, soapy water for washing, the second with hotter, clean water for rinsing. Beatrice set up the tired old Hobart dish sanitizer for the last run of the day, with a batch of fresh water, then popped on the gas burner to heat the water and grabbed a quick cig out back while the water reached the right temperature.

And then they were off. Claire worked her way from the front and Doris from the back. Beatrice kept busy in the middle, first gathering and cleaning dishes, pots, and utensils then cleaning all surfaces that grubby hands could touch—chairs, walls, counters, and windows—and bathrooms.

Then, working together, they scrubbed, washed, and put away all the utensils in their proper places, and lastly, Claire stacked the chairs on the dozen small tables and went after the floor with a mop and bucket. She ended by filling the salt-and-pepper shakers, reloading the napkin dispensers, and topping off the bottles of ketchup while Beatrice and Doris checked the food inventory, planning for the next day's menu.

That menu would be no mystery and as regular as the calendar. The following day was Thursday, so that meant lasagna and fresh-baked bread would lead the menu as the only rotating item, followed by the usual suspects of eggs all day—any style—pancakes and bacon or sausages for breakfast, hamburgers on homemade buns for lunch. They'd serve caramel rolls the size of an outstretched hand at five thirty in the morning until they were gone and homemade pie made from whatever fruit was easiest to get from eleven o'clock until it was gone.

"Here ya go." Doris handed Beatrice the list of stuff she liked to get locally and not from the big food-delivery trucks. "If you see Bob from the locker, tell him he's got a deal on that bacon. It cured up nice, and he sliced it right. Tell him I'm good for five sides a week, maybe more." Beatrice nodded and headed out to her dilapidated Chevy wagon. She and Doris would meet back at the café about eight o'clock to do the final prep work. Claire was usually not required for that and, as the new person, not yet welcome.

Doris turned and eyed Claire. "See ya tomorrow, five thirty." On impulse, she brusquely brushed Claire's cheek with a callused thumb. "Get some sleep. You look a little ill." That was about as close to a warm embrace as Doris ever came.

Claire nodded and walked out the back, sticking to the shadow of the cinder-block building, a faded jean jacket in her hand. Hard to believe the cool of the morning has boiled into this—not much cooler than the kitchen, just windier. She absentmindedly flicked a grasshopper off the rough wall before leaning back against it. The damn things were everywhere this year. The breeze dried the sweat that dampened her uniform. Her legs trembled slightly with fatigue, and her feet ached.

I should get some better shoes. She fingered the tip money in her pocket and looked down at the thin-soled, flat canvas shoes, performing the continuing calculus of needs and wants that people on the edge of poverty do.

The idle thinking stopped immediately when she heard it. In a split second, she was tense and alert, ears straining for the identification and location of the sound.

Fatigue and poverty forgotten, Claire crouched low against the wall. It was a motorcycle definitely. She backtracked quickly to the café's back entry. Locked. *Shit.* The sound of the motorcycle was louder now—not racing, just burbling along, the very sound terrifying her.

Better move. She picked a direction and walked briskly, head down. Her apartment was down the alley about a block and a half away.

She was almost there when the chopper appeared suddenly. Her glance upward was met perfectly by the casual gaze of the rider. He was idling along, but he stopped immediately, giving her a look of shocked recognition.

It was Purp. Frozen in place, she could only look into his mournful gaze.

"Please…" The single word came out as a whisper. There was no way he could have heard it but no way he didn't know what she was asking.

In a brief moment that seemed to stretch on, he sat in the saddle, studying her. Then his shoulders slumped a little, and he nodded once, briefly, like he had made a decision. Goosing the throttle, he continued down the empty street, accelerating.

With Purp out of sight, Claire stood still, listening to the roar of the bike gathering speed as it headed out of town. Her thoughts were far away from the café and the town of Dansing, and a low, trilling hum of fear replaced the dull ache of fatigue in her belly.

They found me.

About the author

JJ Gould lived throughout the plains states working in radio, advertising, and funeral service. He now lives Zihuatenejo, Mexico where he writes sporadically and lives continually with his wife, Libby and their Irish Setter, Dauntless. Readers can find him on Facebook or can schedule speaking engagements with him. He is currently working on the third book in the *Dead Air* series: *Dead End*, which will be released in November of 2017

40003844R00153

Made in the USA
Lexington, KY
23 May 2019